SALEM'S
ROPES

Inspired by the True Story of the
Haunted Ropes Mansion

Andrina,

JOSEPH C. GIOCONDA

"After the first glass, you see things as you wish they were. After the second, you see things as they are not. Finally, you see things as they really are, and that is the most horrible thing in the world."
– Oscar Wilde

SALEM'S ROPES

Based on the True Story of the Haunted Ropes Mansion

Copyright © 2021 Joseph C. Gioconda

This book is a work of fiction. Many names, characters, places, and incidents are the product of the author's imagination or are used fictitiously to build a believable world. For story purposes, the author altered the timeline of historical events but attempted to stay as close to the truth as possible.

ISBN: 978-1-7372860-5-9 (Paperback)

ISBN: 978-1-7372860-6-6 (Hardcover)

Library of Congress Cataloguing-in-Publication Data

Front cover image by C5 Designs II

Printed by IngramSpark and Amazon

First printed edition August 2021

Published by Newtown IP Holdings LLC
301 South State Street, Suite 102S
Newtown PA 18940

www.SalemsRopes.com

CONTENTS

FOREWORD

Salem's Ropes contains profanity as well as violent imagery and occult text that some may consider offensive.

Acknowledgements

I would like to thank the Trustees of the Peabody Essex Museum who keep the Ropes Mansion and Gardens beautiful.

I also want to thank a fellow author, my wife Alison, for keeping an eye on our children Luke and Morgan while I disappeared at night to complete this book.

GALLOWS

Sweaty, George took a swig from his water bottle. He wiped his brow while stretching on a stone wall near a baseball diamond in the park. He had just run a solid five miles and planned on walking home to cool off.

A woman in a black dress sat on a bench nearby. She looked pale and gaunt and had scraggly, matted gray hair. He assumed she was a homeless woman feeding pigeons, but her black gown seemed out of place.

"Hot out, huh?" he said.

She muttered something that wasn't in English.

"I'm sorry?" he said.

"Proctor's Ledge," she mumbled.

"I'm sorry, I just moved here from Chicago, I'm not familiar—"

"—the gallows," she said, pointing upward.

"Oh yeah?" he asked, not knowing what she was talking about.

"Do you live nearby?" he asked.

"We never left," she said, staring into the sky.

"Uh, nice meeting you," he said awkwardly. He turned to jog back on the bike path away from her.

After a few seconds, he turned his head to look back, and she was gone. He stopped dead in his tracks and turned around. There was nowhere that she could have gone. There was no other path and only dense woods in both directions.

"Hello?"

Silence.

That night, he woke up abruptly at 3:30 a.m. In his nightmare, he was at the park again. However, the sky was neither day nor night. On the branches of trees overhead were numerous bodies hanging in nooses, swaying slightly from side to side as the breeze moved them. Their legs dangled above him.

He stared up. He recognized his family. Their eyes were bulging and lifeless. His wife Giselle dangled from one branch with her high heeled shoe having fallen off. His daughter was swaying on another, wearing her tiny pink sneakers. One of the corpses looked up and gurgled, "These are the ropes. Your ropes." It was the old woman who had been perched on the park bench.

DECISION

"What they do with Halloween decorations and costumes here, it's incredible. Melissa's going to love it." Giselle and George strolled along the waterfront which extended from Salem to Juniper Point past Dead Horse Beach. Tourist shops, arcades and kitschy attractions were stacked next to one another along the boardwalk.

"She better," Giselle replied. "After pulling her out of third grade, she's going to miss her friends. She skipped the first three weeks of school already."

The couple stared out at the boats bobbing on the water. Their daughter ran ahead.

"I still can't believe you bought a house without me seeing it first. What did you get us into?" Giselle said.

"Just wait until you see it in person. It's gorgeous," he bragged, as Melissa dashed down the wooden pier of Salem's Neck.

Even before they saw their new home, he had decided to give them a quick sightseeing tour of the area. They grabbed a couple of hot dogs.

"It's just different here," he said. Melissa was talking to a fisherman and staring into his pail of fish.

"Be careful, honey!" Giselle shouted.

"I feel more alive here than I've felt in years." He held their golden retriever's leash as the dog sniffed at the fish in the metal bucket. "Bailey, get your snout out of there," he laughed.

Giselle saw his eyes sparkle. She was surprised to see him this way again. It was something she hadn't seen or felt since before their daughter was born; maybe even before. It reminded her of why she'd fallen in love with him in the first place, a reason she almost had forgotten.

"Come on, Mel, let's go!" Giselle shouted. She wanted to see their new house during daylight. They had shipped their belongings separately, but the moving truck wouldn't arrive for two more days.

When she saw the sign for the microbrewery, she grimaced. She wondered if he had unconsciously—or even consciously— chosen a house near one. He'd been stone cold sober since before they were married, but she also knew that temptation was always lurking. He'd also made it a practice to drink seltzer anytime he had a craving for a beer, and it had worked. He lost thirty pounds, started working out and never looked back.

When they pulled up in front of 318 Essex Street, Giselle's mouth fell open.

"They call it a Georgian colonial. It's got real character," he said, as they stepped out. "It's called the Ropes Mansion. It was built in the 1720s, even before the United States was... the United States. It's now the Lawson residence. Or maybe we can call it the Lawson Mansion," he smiled proudly.

As they stepped out of their double-parked electric car, he explained that the house, although altered through the years and recently restored, looked very much like its original form. It was stark white, with jet black shutters and roof. A metal white picket-style fence surrounded the entire property, with finials on columnar pillars adding to the dramatic frontage. A white flagpole was mounted above the front door, but no flag currently hung on the vacant house. It looked like the White House on a smaller scale. The gardens were lush and large.

"Wow," Giselle said flatly.

"That's it? *Wow?*"

Giselle could sense apprehension in his voice while they stood, keys to their new home dangling nervously in his hand. He had made a major life decision without consulting her. If she exhibited anything less than enthusiasm, it would crush his spirit. Not to mention that he'd already bought it and they were in contract on their house back home. She had to make it work, even it wasn't her first choice.

"It's really...something," she said. "Very different from Matthew's Circle back home, that's for sure."

"Back home? This is home now."

"It's...beautiful George," she said. "I can't wait to see inside."

In their Chicago home back on the Fourth of July, Giselle had nearly dropped a dinner plate into the sink when he announced that he'd bought a house in Salem during a business trip.

"You're kidding?" she'd said incredulously.

George had beamed as he opened his brown leather satchel and scrambled inside to pull out a sheaf of papers. He dangled them in front of her face. She grabbed at them, but he drew them back. He signaled that he couldn't let her touch them with her wet, soapy hands which were still clad in yellow latex gloves.

She had squinted her big blue eyes for a closer look and blown her brown bangs from her face.

In his hands were a bunch of signed forms from moving companies and a document that said 'Deed of Title' written in printed calligraphy.

"You weren't kidding," she said flatly.

She had expected a logical explanation or excuse, but he had said nothing and just continued to grin. Back when they were first dating at Northwestern, that smile could always get him out of trouble. Like the time he'd messed around with her girlfriend Becky over Memorial Day. He explained they'd both been drunk on tequila, and that smile had gotten him out of big trouble. Not this time.

"You're freaking serious?" she asked, turning around to face him, back to the sink. "I can't believe you're for real."

"It's gonna be great," he had stressed. "I really think you're overreacting."

"Overreacting?" Giselle put both soapy hands on her waist and stared point blank into his stubbled face.

"I haven't even been to Massachusetts! And you bought a house without me even seeing it?!" She grabbed at the papers, not caring if they got wet. This time, he let her take them.

While he was traveling, he had called her at least twice a day to tell her how much he loved Salem and its unique historical aesthetic. He sent her dozens of photos on Messenger and short video clips of him at various places there. He even took smiling selfies with random strangers.

She had thought he was just having a little fun, and she was even happy for him. He needed to blow off some steam and seemed so enthusiastic about the business trip. When he told her that he was on his way back with a surprise, she expected to get an earful, hearing about the beautiful environment and rich history. Maybe a cool T-shirt. But this was too much.

"We're supposed to abandon everything...my job, Melissa's school, sell the house, everything, and just up and move there, because you liked its history? It's crazy, George. Even for you."

He had grabbed the wet papers out of her hand and laid them flat on the kitchen table to dry. He drew a chair and gestured to Giselle to come sit on his lap. She said no and crossed her arms.

"It might just be the kick we need to get our family out of the doldrums," he said.

"George, tell me the truth. Are you drinking again?"

"Absolutely not," he declared.

He had been an electrical engineer for two decades. Even though he ran ten miles a week and played basketball at the gym, he had turned fifty in March, and his retirement was drawing ever closer. His marriage to Giselle was not his first rodeo.

He had separated from Michele eight years before after an unhappy marriage. Amid his ugly divorce, he'd spotted his college girlfriend Giselle working out at the gym. She had everything Michele never did:

energy and a laid-back attitude. Giselle had never been married and had no kids of her own. She was two years younger than him, but looked thirty-five, at most.

Plus, she supported him as an old friend. She stood with him throughout his bruising divorce and bitter custody battle with Michele, which he lost. At least he got bi-weekly visitations with his twin teenage daughters. But his partying had come back to haunt him during the hearing. The family court judge wasn't impressed, and he was disappointed he couldn't talk her into awarding shared custody, or even weekly visitations.

As time went on, he came to feel as though he could no longer live without Giselle, that she was everything he needed. He decided to try for success again. They got married in a little ceremony outside town hall. Just a Justice of the Peace, two witnesses, his two daughters and some friends. Michele did not come or even wish them well.

Since the wedding, his relationship with his daughters had become strained, to say the least. He suspected Michele had bad-mouthed him incessantly to the girls after that. But the twins were old enough to figure it out for themselves. They had graduated college the year before, so he no longer had to pay child support. Long ago, he had agreed to pay for their tuition, which was a brutal expense. But even that had now thankfully come to an end.

Unfortunately, the girls were growing farther and farther away from him. Literally. They had attended school in Southern California and stayed out there after graduation. They traveled a lot, but never visited. He didn't hate his new life, but he always felt like something was missing.

After Melissa was born nine years ago, Giselle and he had decided to buy a relatively impressive new house in a mellow, quiet, and ultimately boring suburb an hour and a half west of Chicago. They got a good deal on a house in a brand-new development with an acre of land and an in-ground pool. After years spent in Chicago's apartments, it felt liberating to breathe fresh air. They even had a horse farm at the end of their street.

But when he sat outside on the back deck to read his iPad and drink seltzer water, he felt as though the silence was squeezing his throat. He and Giselle had moved there to do things differently and learn from their mistakes and give their daughter a better life. But with the years flying by, he'd started to wonder what that really meant.

Melissa had little excitement in her young life. She'd never seen an ocean or the coasts. They just hadn't had the time or inclination to make the trip, since he always had work and she always had gymnastics, dance recitals or other activities keeping them close to home. They'd spent a weekend near Denver once, but she'd been bored without a good wi-fi connection in the cabin.

Perhaps she was still young, but he felt that if they continued living as they did, he would eventually lose Melissa the same way he'd lost his other girls. His trip to historic Massachusetts was enlightening, and he'd made up his mind to change the situation up. He was going to give their lives some spice; they were going to mix it up by moving to the witch capital of the world.

Melissa was more interested in the kids playing on the streets than in the façade or interior of the old house. Halloween was still a month away, but there were already kids in costumes. The house faced a public square, so there was a lot of pedestrian traffic. To the right of the house was a diagonal street with a three-story brick microbrewery. At least a dozen people stood in line out front, presumably for a tour or something.

To the left of the house was another diagonal street leading to the piers, which were only a few blocks away. The dramatic Ropes Mansion stood cattycorner to the public square, so it was a centerpiece and could not be missed. Right next to the house stood an imposing stone church.

George fumbled with the keys to open the front door. The doorknob, brass and heavily dented, looked antique. The locks had already been changed by the realtor and this one was sticking. Giselle stood at the bottom of the stairs, waiting for him to open the door. She was looking up at the dingy white curtains hanging in a window on the second floor.

"Honey is the real estate agent meeting us?" she asked.

"No. Why? We already closed on it."

"Oh, I just thought I saw someone move the curtain," she said.

"Nope, just us."

He pushed a little harder and the front door opened. The three of them stepped into the foyer of their new home.

SETTLEMENT

"You have to see the weird stuff I found in the basement," George said excitedly. "I think the last owners left a bunch of crates." They'd been in their new home for a week, and there was still a ton of unpacking to do. The movers had left cardboard boxes scattered all over, even in the basement.

Many of the furnishings they owned were stylistically out of place. George had already gotten rid of several pieces of black lacquered furniture on Craigslist that he'd unfortunately paid to truck halfway across the country. But he was glad to be rid of them, as he could foresee the couple finding enjoyment in buying smaller antiques that would better fit the classic colonial style.

"I'll look later. I gotta get the rest of the laundry done and get Melissa to bed. Why don't you go say hi to your daughter?" She gestured into the formal living room where the girl was laying on the couch in front of the fireplace wearing headphones, silently watching YouTube videos on a pink tablet.

Giselle went back to doing the laundry, shaking her head. The laundry room was on the first floor in an old servant's parlor off the kitchen, and it was cramped, at least compared to back home. The dining room was lined with cupboards to display china that they did not own.

George kissed his daughter on the head. She didn't even look up. "Hi, Daddy."

"Are you enjoying the new house?" he asked.

"Yep," she said, unconvincingly.

"We can go shopping this weekend for new bedroom furniture, Ok? Maybe you'd like a nice daybed."

"Ok," she replied. He had expected her to be more enthusiastic.

"Well, hello to you too, Bailey." The dog barely lifted its head in interest.

George sprinted up the narrow creaking stairs into the master bathroom to shower and change after work. He had gotten a new job easily at a civil engineering firm in Boston, only thirty minutes away by train. He could make it there in twenty by car, in no traffic.

As hot water from the shower ran down his muscular back, he couldn't stop thinking about Salem and the history of the house. He was sure his family would grow to love it once they learned more.

After he'd dried his black and gray pepper hair, he laid in bed holding his iPad, reading about Salem, its history, and its witches. A museum of witchcraft was literally right down the block. He couldn't wait to check it out, although it was already tough to get a ticket this time of year.

After only a week, he had already become so fascinated with the subject, he decided he might even try writing a book about the house. He could research and write about the witch trials of Salem as his own form of tribute. Maybe he needed a creative outlet to get to know the place better, he thought, as he started to doze off. He could also meet more locals that way.

He didn't hear Giselle enter their room. He jolted awake when he felt a wet tongue rolling playfully around his earlobe. He knew what that meant. Melissa was asleep. He and Giselle hadn't had sex in a while, as they were getting too lazy in their life and the move had been exhausting. He lifted her off the ground and placed her gently on the bed, then he made sure to lock the door behind him. She slipped off her silk pajamas. That night felt like it'd be different from other nights, and he didn't want to wake Melissa up.

After, Giselle took a quick shower before bed. Before, he'd been ready to fall asleep, but now he felt reinvigorated. He opened the bathroom door a crack and whispered to her that he was going downstairs for a bit. She nodded.

He went downstairs quietly so he wouldn't wake his daughter. He walked into the living room. The cable television hadn't been hooked up yet. Even though it was only Thursday, it was noisy outside. A group of boisterous college kids were lined up to get into the microbrewery, even at this late hour.

He decided to go back down into the basement to explore some more. For the first time, he noticed that the small horizontal windows of the basement were painted shut, their glass panes blacked out. No light from the outside came in. The basement had two incandescent light bulbs, and one fluorescent bar which gave off a strange glow and a hum. As an engineer, he would enjoy spending some time wiring up brighter LED lights throughout to give some proper lighting to the dark, shadowy rooms down.

In every cellar he'd ever been in since he was a kid, there had been concrete slab floors. Sometimes, friends' basements were finished, and hard synthetic carpeting was glued down over it. But there, the floor was fine brown dirt. Just real earth that could be dug up.

On one side was a large stone hearth with a small chimney that was connected to the fireplaces upstairs. It must have been used for cooking, as rusty iron metal bars were affixed to the rear of it to hold pots.

The walls of the foundation consisted of flat gray stones. Slate layers were fastened together with centuries of hard beige mortar. George knew that the stony foundations had fully settled, and any moisture that had permeated them was long dried up. He walked past several rows of cardboard boxes full of Melissa's clothes stacked toward the rear of the cellar, waiting to be unpacked. There was no light at all back there, so he grabbed a small penlight that was lying near the boiler.

One wall was no more than hardened cement. Clearly, a wall that had been placed there more recently, at least within the last century or so. It was made of concrete and had a few small pebbles in it. He knew that around the turn of the twentieth century, workers sometimes used small rocks to help hold cement together. But he wondered why workers would have lugged dense materials down there to fashion an interior wall. After curing, the cement would have become heavy and practically impenetrable.

A few days before, he'd noticed a few small symbols carved into the cement that he wanted to show Giselle. He hadn't recognized them, but when he was a boy, his grandfather Walter had given him an old Masonic Bible that had been in his family for a long time. He vaguely remembered seeing weird symbols inscribed at the front of the book that seemed similar.

That would make sense, he thought to himself. *This place has been here for hundreds of years. Freemasons may very well have built much of Salem, and they might have left little fingerprints in their stonework be-hind.* Next time he was down here with his iPhone, he would snap some photos and maybe post them to Reddit to see if anyone recognized them.

He glanced up at the rafters. The header beam was made of a long, thick round log. It looked petrified and had turned gray. He recognized axe marks and knots on it. It had once been a very large tree. It had been there for centuries, holding up the house and people above it all that time. Its length traversed the entire house, from one side of the rock foundation to the other. In the center, he noticed a few strands of dry old hemp rope. As he stared up, he tripped, nearly falling on his face.

Parts of the dirt floor had been dug up, leaving holes that were at least two foot wide and a foot deep. Were they sinkholes where the foundation had settled? They looked too circular; they appeared dug out by hand, and they had no apparent connection to the foundation of the house itself. The next time he went to Home Depot or Lowes, he'd need to pick up a few bags of small rocks and soil to fill them in. Otherwise, someone might fall and break a rib, or worse.

He continued to explore the four rear rooms of the large basement. The prior owners had left a dozen wooden crates in the corners, which the couple would have to go through once they'd unpacked their own moving boxes. There were ancient cobwebs everywhere.

One of the crates had a big black letter X scrawled across it in paint. Inside were a variety of odd brass objects that looked like they had come from a church. George had been raised Catholic and had even once been an altar boy. He found Mass boring, but he liked to serve at weddings and funerals for the tips. He found that tips at a funeral could be as high at twenty dollars. But he was never religious.

He recognized one of the items in the crate as an incense burner which his parish priest Father Fullum had called a "censer." He always thought that was funny, as the word sounded a lot like "censor." He also recognized a thurible and a paten. *But why would old Roman Catholic objects be in this basement?* Right next door was a First Unitarian Church. Most likely, it had never been a Catholic Church. These items could be Episcopalian, he thought, putting them back.

Another one of the crates contained a few green glass bottles. He picked one up. The bottle had a yellowed ceramic stopper on top, attached by a decorative, swing-top lid. In the hand-blown green glass was a symbol he didn't recognize, with the elaborate letters 'S' and 'R'. There was no telling what was once inside of it.

He carefully placed it upright on a wooden shelf nearby. The other crates had rusty locks, and odds and ends inside, and he would enjoy going through them. Several very old oil paintings with battered gold frames were propped up, facing the wall. Their surfaces were heavily cracked in spots, but they were clearly originals and vintage. He pulled two paintings out and lugged them upstairs where he could see them better once he'd turned on the kitchen lights.

The first was the profile of an unsmiling woman (a grandmother, perhaps), who was seated in a chair. She was wearing a black dress which faded into the background of the painting. Her white collar stood out in contrast. Underneath the painting was a small, engraved brass plate that said 'Sarah Putnam Ropes, 1893'.

The other painting was of a different woman. The brass engraving underneath said 'Mary Pickman Ropes', and the painting displayed a similarly morose woman who had a similar dress with white ribbing on the collar. The women appeared to be sisters.

He set them aside in the kitchen pantry to show Giselle in the morning. He suspected she wouldn't be in love with the idea of displaying rather grim-looking old women on the walls of their house. However, they were clearly part of its long history, and deserved a place of honor and respect, he thought. He also made a note to himself to do a Google search for the two names.

SAMHAIN

"The Celts called it Samhain," Sherri Donaldson told her class, looking over her eyeglasses. "Does anyone know what day I'm talking about?"

The class cried in unison: "Halloween!"

Melissa hadn't known the answer, but she smiled. The other kids were excited about the holiday party Ms. Donaldson and other students' parents had planned. Each year, the third graders at Witchcraft Heights Elementary School on Frederick Street held the best Halloween party in school. They hosted a parade that marched around the block, while parents and others took photos. They even got the rest of the day off, which was spent trick or treating with parents, siblings, and friends in the Halloween capital of the world.

George stood outside on his steps with a mug of hot coffee. He'd taken the day off. This year, Halloween fell on a Friday. By morning, the square had already become rowdy and noisy. While he could not wait for the night's festivities to start, it was a bit too much for George so early in the day, and he decided to venture back inside and have a moment of quiet. He had wanted to sit outside on the steps and share in the atmosphere, but there was only so much noise and music he could take after he'd just woken up. Inside, he grabbed a book to keep himself occupied.

By mid-afternoon, the turnout was huge. Just looking out the side bay window, he could see scores of people lined up in all sorts of costumes, most of them witch-related, and they had all gathered and queued to visit Madhouse Microbrewery.

In their kitchen, Melissa was in a rush to go back outside to trick or treat, as she didn't want to be left out of the festivities after the school parade had ended. She'd dressed up as one of the witches from a cartoon show on television. George didn't know exactly which character it was, or what show it was from, and he didn't care, as he was much too impressed with how cute his little girl looked.

He gloated over her for a while, and then stuffed her plastic pumpkin with candy he had gotten secretly and a fifty-dollar bill, as she prepared to go trick or treating with all her new school friends. She wanted to squeal and jump on him in happiness, but he put a finger to his lips and whispered at her to shush. The gifts were a little secret between him and her.

This was part of what George had wanted for his daughter: a fun active life, friends, festivals, holidays, candy. Everything that a kid her age could want in a vibrant town. It wasn't like they didn't have Halloween back in the Midwest, nor was it as if Melissa didn't have friends, but it was never like this. Halloween was mostly just cheesy lawn decorations, and trick or treating only happened at the mall, if at all.

But this, this place, finally had the vibe he'd been looking for. The pedestrians were already dressed in the wildest outfits one could think of. Finding one wouldn't even be a problem at the many costume shops lining the streets.

"Mel! Don't forget your witch hat!" Giselle walked into the kitchen holding up a pointy witch hat. George stared at her, taken aback. Even Giselle was in the Halloween spirit, dressed up as the comic villain, Poison Ivy. George knew *her*, at least. She pulled the look off perfectly well, and she looked extremely sexy in those green tights, especially with the way the V-neck pushed up her breasts. George's only issue was that it might catch the eyes of other men and attract unnecessary attention to her, but he wasn't going to tell her that. He didn't have to worry about it, either. Giselle could take care of herself.

They stepped outside. George was about to talk when Giselle interrupted him. "I have to stay with Mel and the kids while they go trick or treating." She kissed him on the cheek and knocked him out of his thoughts. "We'll be back before it's too dark. Try not to hurt anyone

17

while you're at it." She finished, noticing that he seemed a bit concerned about her outfit and the men already staring at her from the crowd on the street.

"There are bags of Snickers and Kit Kats by the door, but only give out one at a time, or else we'll run out," she said. He nodded. A group of rowdy high schoolers were already walking up to their front door.

Giselle and Melissa left to join a group of younger schoolkids down the street. A little further along, she was joined by another young woman, whom George guessed was a mother of one of the kids with them. He watched, standing by the front door, his mind completely blank. He was suddenly knocked back to reality by someone in the crowd playing a trumpet very lousily as they walked toward his front door to demand more candy.

Young adults and teenagers were now using his front lawn as a hangout, chugging beers, and getting drunk. He gave them a few pieces of candy and shooed them away. A few laughed at him. Some of them hailing him for being bold enough to live in the Ropes Mansion, which they were calling the 'Madhouse'. He scooted them out of the fenced part of the yard, but he couldn't chase their sneers and comments out of his head.

Since they'd moved in, he'd overheard a few kids refer to their home as the Madhouse. He'd never taken it seriously until now. He'd decided once already to check on the reason they kept calling it that, but it had always slipped his mind.

Now seemed like the right time to find out. When he'd closed on the house, the seller had left him with a small book written by a historian in the 1970s about the property. He went and found it and sat in his favorite leather chair to wait by the door for more kids to ring the doorbell for candy and see if he could find a few minutes in between doorbell rings to read.

The author detailed historical records of all those who had lived in the house from the time it was built in the early 1720s, the era accounting for its striking colonial design. In 1768, Judge Nathaniel Ropes Jr. purchased the house from the merchant Samuel Barnard's nephew. The

Ropes family then moved in and inhabited the house until the early twentieth century, specifically from 1907, making them the custodians of the house for well over a century and thus earning it the name 'Ropes Mansion'.

In the same year, 1907, the house was then given to the Trustees of the Ropes Memorial for public benefit. The house had even featured in the 1993 film *Hocus Pocus*. It was well known in the area. Over the two decades previous, it had become available for use as a residential home, and George and his family were now the ones now living in it. The last owners were an elderly couple. He assumed they'd moved to Florida to retire or something like that.

George liked the history of Salem and its antiquities, but he was still looking for something more than just the previous owners' names. He was looking for some reason why it was being called the Madhouse. After a while, he put the book down to take a walk to see the festivities in the square. He left a bucket full of candy on the front stoop with a handwritten piece of paper that said: 'Take only one!'

He called for Bailey and attached his leash. They went out the back door and locked it, the key sticking in the lock.

"Damn it," he said, struggling with the lock. The dog yanked on the chain as kids went by.

He retrieved his key and walked down the street toward the microbrewery. The line was so long and wide that he had to walk in the street to get past the hordes of costumed college kids waiting to get in.

"Excuse me," he said, the dog sniffing them.

"Cute dog, mister," a couple of the kids said.

"Thanks. Cute costumes," he replied.

He started to walk down the street. There were a staggering number of people standing in front of the Madhouse Microbrewery. He had never noticed that the sign in front was engraved in wood with a font that suggested chaos, and in the background of the sign was an etched image of his own house.

DRINKS

After he passed the brewery's mobbed entrance, he saw a modest, dilapidated shack next to it that he hadn't noticed before. 'Salem's Ropes Tonic," the flimsy red painted sign above the rusty screen door said.

"Care for one?" asked an elderly man, seated on a cheap green lawn chair with frayed webbing. "Here," he said, popping the metal clasp to release the ceramic topper. The bottle looked familiar. On the front was a cheap paper label that displayed a noose. The man was handing the bottles out to trick-or-treaters in place of candy. Some kids refused them.

"Oh, thanks old timer," George said, taking the bottle from him.

"I'm Tim Eden, pull up a seat," he said, offering George another ratty lawn chair. "Watch the nut parade."

"Thanks, don't mind if I do, Tim." George tied off the dog who had lain down on the sidewalk.

"Let me get him some water." The old man pulled out a round, metal dog dish that was next to the chairs and poured some water out of a plastic bottle into it. The dog lapped it up.

"Nice to meet you," Tim said, extending his calloused hand.

"I'm George Lawson. This miserable guy here is Bailey." He ruffled the dog's ears.

George sipped the water which was tinged green in color from the bottle. He grimaced. "Ah... thanks."

It was relatively tasteless at first, like flavored carbonated water of some kind. But as the first few gulps went down his throat, the bitter and terrible aftertaste hit. George, caught off guard, coughed and gagged.

20

"Terrible, right?" Tim laughed.

"Uh, no, it's just…different. I'm a big fan of sparkling water, what is this?"

Tim laughed. "My family bottled this recipe when we settled here a long, long time ago. It's never changed one bit. Was way before Coca Cola. But it grows on ya, you'll see."

George wasn't convinced, but he took another little sip. "This bottle, I think I saw one in my basement. It was a little different."

"We've been recycling since before we had to. You're new here. You in the Ropes' place, right?"

"Yeah, with my wife Giselle and my daughter Melissa. We just moved in last month."

"How you likin' it?" Tim asked, sipping some water from the plastic bottle.

"It's great. Big difference from Chicago."

"Ah, the Windy City," said Tim. "Never been there, but I imagine it's a long way from here." He glanced at some high school kids decked out in goth gear walking down the street.

"We got tired of it there, wanted to change it up a bit, ya know?"

"Oh, it's a big change all right," said Tim. "This place has always had its share of weirdos. Especially in the sixties. You can't imagine. Hippie central. Today, it's mostly teen punks and college kids. They come down from Boston to make a mess. We're just townies."

George laughed. He sipped Tim's homemade tonic again and wished he had some of the dog's bowl water to wash it down.

"Your Ropes there, and their mansion, very long and peculiar history," said Tim, handing out two more bottles of his drink from a cooler to trick-or-treaters.

Before he could complete the thought, he interrupted himself.

"That reminds me. Have you met Marlena?" asked Tim.

"Marlena? No."

"Come here, let me introduce you two," he chuckled. Tim stood up slowly, holding his back. "Leave Bailey here, he'll be fine." The dog looked up at George.

"Ok, be right back." George patted the dog.

They walked toward the brewery. The line to get in was now snaking around the corner. Standing near the front door was a very attractive woman in her early thirties. She was wearing a cat costume, with cat ears and whiskers painted on. Her green eyes were heavily covered with mascara, and her bleached blonde hair reached past her shoulders. She had an oval-shaped face and hips that were hugged by her black tights. Her eyes squinted as she smiled, and her short, pointed nose had a black dot on it from the Halloween make-up.

George was a little worried that he'd make her uncomfortable if she caught him looking her up and down like that.

"Marlena, come here." Tim waved towards her.

She yelled out to one of her employees to take her clipboard, then walked towards him. His heartbeat increased.

"Hi, Tim!" She greeted the old man cheerfully, giving him a big kiss on his cheek and then rubbing off the scarlet red lipstick stain she'd left.

"Marlena, this is George. Just moved into the Ropes."

"Hi, George." She extended her hand, which was clad in a black fingerless glove to match the costume.

"Nice to meet you," he said.

"How long have you been in there?" She gestured toward the mansion.

"Almost a month now. Well over a month," he said.

"Wow, I feel bad I haven't seen you or introduced myself. This is my place," she said, pointing up at the hanging wooden sign that said Madhouse Brewery.

"If you want, I could give you a tour. No tickets, on the house. Consider it my apology for not welcoming you personally to the neighborhood after all this time."

"Nah that's okay. You have nothing to apologize for. I should have been the one to say hi, if anything," he said.

But she insisted. She even promised to give him a few free drinks if he came along.

He considered it only for a split second. "I don't drink…anymore but thank you."

"I'm sorry to hear that," she said, making a sad face.

"No, really, it's Ok. Just got a little out of hand, that's all."

"And now you live in the Madhouse?" She giggled. "Oh, don't mind me. I'd live in the Ropes myself if I could afford it. It's too bad that you quit partying. We could've had a blast."

There was an awkward silence.

A high school kid dressed up as the Grim Reaper walked up to Tim at that moment and asked for one of his tonic bottles. The student seemed familiar with him and their exchange was casual. George watched Tim walk back to the shack to take one from his cooler for him.

"Well, I'll take you up on that offer sometime, but I have to get back home," said George.

"Wife and kids?" she asked, grabbing his hand, and holding it up to see the gold wedding band.

"Yep, you got it," she said. "I was just out walking the dog, and met Tim."

"Some other time, then," she said, smiling.

"Definitely," he said, smiling as well and walking back to grab Bailey's leash.

"How about one for the road?" Tim asked George, as he held out a tonic bottle in his hand.

"Uh, sure." George took it graciously, smiling.

When he walked in the back door with Bailey, Melissa and Giselle had just come in the front.

"Your daughter is too much," said Giselle, exasperated. She plopped down on the couch.

"Why, what did she do now?" he asked, chuckling.

"For one, she wandered off with her new friends without telling me."

George's face got serious. "Melissa, what did we talk about? This is a city, not a cul-de-sac. There are thousands of people walking around here we don't know. Plus, this is Halloween – a lot of drunks and crazies are out tonight."

"I thought we moved here because it was fun," said the girl.

"Yes, fun is one thing, but we have to be safe, right?"

"Ok," she said glumly. "Whatever."

"What is that?" Giselle pointed to the green glass bottle on the kitchen table. "That's not a beer, is it? It looks like Grolsch."

Giselle got up and walked over to the bottle. She opened it, sniffed at it cautiously then pulled away. She stuck her tongue out in disgust.

"Blech. What is this?"

"Some local soda. It's non-alcoholic but it's an acquired taste, I guess. It's growing on me."

Giselle shook her head. "Better brush your teeth before you come to bed with that mouth or you'll be sleeping outside. Don't give any of it to Melissa and keep it the hell away from me."

"Yeah, I don't even think Bailey would drink it," he joked.

After Melissa went to bed, George sat up watching a horror movie marathon that was playing on cable television for Halloween.

Bailey was pawing at the door to the basement.

"Want to go for a walk?" George asked him.

The golden retriever looked up at George and went back to nosing at the bottom of the basement door.

"I'll get ya something to eat, ok?" George whispered, as he stood up to get food and water for his bowl. Bailey ignored the fresh food and water and kept whining and staring up at the closed door.

"What is it buddy?" he asked, scratching the dog's ears. Bailey just whined louder.

"You want to go down? Catching mice is for cats, remember?" he chuckled.

But as he opened the door, the dog took off in the other direction. George thought he saw movement and heard a box in the basement shift.

"Hello? Is someone down there?" he called out down the stairs.

He turned on the light switch. "Is someone there?" he asked again, more forcefully.

He picked up a Maglite that was on the stairwell's ledge and pointed the light beam down the stairs. He descended each step slowly, pointing the flashlight's beam all over the walls of the rooms. There was no one to see and nowhere anyone could have come from or gone.

He walked back up the stairs and turned the basement lights back out and locked the basement door with a heavy latch.

"Nothing down there, buddy," he said to Bailey, who was hiding under the kitchen table, shivering. "You're watching too many scary movies too," he said to the dog jokingly.

George flopped back down on the couch to watch television, and munch on more tortilla chips.

He heard a loud three raps at the front door. He turned the television off with the remote.

"Jesus Christ, it's 3 a.m., more trick or treaters?" he said under his breath. He grabbed the last remaining bucket of candy and went to open the front door. "A little late for candy—"

He opened the front door, but no one was there. He stepped outside and looked all around. No one was in sight.

He went back inside the house and closed the door.

The basement door was wide open.

"Giselle?"

He walked over to the basement door and closed it again.

"Bailey?" The dog was nowhere to be found and the food and water were undisturbed.

He thought he heard a child's small voice in the living room.

"Melissa?" He said as he walked into the living room, but no one was in there.

CAMBRIDGE

"This house is weird, I'm telling you," whispered George while sipping sparkling water and reading his iPad while standing in the kitchen at the granite countertop in the morning. "I had some strange stuff happen last night."

Giselle shot him an annoyed glance. "Melissa is in the living room, she doesn't need to hear that," she whispered.

"Sorry," he said under his breath. "But I don't think I'm imagining it. I mean, you know I watch too many scary movies but still."

"Tell me later, I'm running late," she said, putting down her coffee mug on the counter. "I have to get Mel to school and get to work. We were both almost late yesterday. You off today?"

"Yep," George said. "Driving into Boston."

"Can you pick me up some chowdah?" joked Giselle, mocking the local accent. "Seriously, stop at Faneuil Hall and get me some with oystah crackers. I will heat it up tonight."

"You'll put on ten times the calories you'll burn today," he patted her toned butt.

"Nice," she said sarcastically.

Melissa had settled into her elementary school routine after a few weeks, and Giselle had found a part-time job at the gym anticipating the increased number of new memberships around the New Year.

George was making it a practice to take a few personal days off from work and spend them researching the tragedies that had supposedly occurred in the house. Last week, he had stopped by the Historical Society and chatted with Ms. Ratliff, the curator. Much of the information that he received from her was redundant to what he already knew. Local history books just repeated the refrain: The house had been passed down since it was built in 1720 from one Ropes generation to the next and an unusual number of deaths had occurred in the house.

One tidbit caught his attention, though. The curator had casually mentioned that the part of Essex Street where the house was located was particularly old and had been settled even before the Ropes house was first built in 1720. Some structure may have existed on the site as far back as 1639, when the first Puritan Church in Salem was founded right next door. He wasn't sure how to research that far back, but he was fascinated that his property could have been consistently occupied for nearly four hundred years.

Certainly, in Europe, that type of timeframe was commonplace. When he had visited London on a backpacking trip in college, he remembered how a "new bridge" there could have been built eight hundred years ago. But still, living in a house with that kind of history was intoxicating. He had to learn more.

He drove to Cambridge and parked in a lot next to the University. He plugged in his electric car and walked past the bookstores that sold countless Harvard t-shirts to tourists as well as proud parents and students. He had scheduled a meeting with Professor Christopher, who taught a graduate school class in the history of Salem including its architecture.

"Professor?" George knocked on an old wooden door that was partially open.

"Yes?" asked a hunched over, bearded gray-haired man in his seventies wearing glasses.

"Yes, hi," George said, as he entered the office. It was cluttered and decked out in all kinds of architectural prints and photographs. "I'm George Lawson. Thank you for meeting with me."

"No problem. I hear you're a Northwestern guy?"

"Yeah, I got my engineering degree there," said George, sitting down.

"Great school," said the professor, turning off his computer screen to face his desk which was piled high with loose papers and books.

"Yep, I loved it. I met my wife there, well, my second wife Giselle."

"Cool deal," said the professor anachronistically, given his age and stature.

"I wanted to ask you some questions about Salem. We recently moved here from Chicago, and bought the Ropes Mansion, have you heard of it?"

"I practically wrote my dissertation on it, what was it...forty-five years ago now. They sold it? Last I remember, it was a museum," the professor said.

"Yeah, I bought it from an older couple. I'm not sure if they bought it when it first went private in the nineties, but yeah, we live in it now. My wife and our daughter Melissa. There's a brewery next door now."

"No kidding," he chuckled. "I assume you know the house's history?" asked the professor.

"Some of it," George replied.

"Did you know it before you bought it?" the professor asked him.

George paused. "Um, not really. I knew it had a lot of local historical significance, but I sorta bought it on a whim. I was out here at a week-long conference at BU, and I guess mid-life crisis kicked in. Most guys buy a convertible, I bought an expensive old mansion."

"Not just any mansion, of course. The Ropes," he said, as he stood up and walked over to a cluttered bookshelf. This is my dissertation, from the 70's, he said, dusting it off. "This is one of my only copies so please return it when you're done."

He handed him a tightly bound book titled Salem's Madhouse by Laurence Christopher.

"I better not let my wife see this," George said, looking at the cover and flipping it open.

"Oh, your wife doesn't know?"

"Not really," he said. "I bought it without telling her," George said, looking up briefly.

"Wow, you Northwestern guys are impetuous," the professor joked. "And here I thought engineers were scared of their own shadows."

"Yeah, well," George said, a little embarrassed. "I usually do more diligence. I was wandering the streets after my conference ended, and I stumbled on a real estate agent's open house. I fell in love with the place, its ambience, everything. I made a ridiculous bid right on the spot, over asking price. A week later, I closed on it. Wiped out my entire 401(k) to pay in cash before we even sold our house in Chicago. I never even had it inspected or did a title search. Really smart Northwestern guy, huh?"

"Well, if it's any consolation, that house is one of the great mysteries of Salem," the professor said, sitting back down and leaning back in his wooden chair. "Back when I was a grad student here in the Classics department, we used to take a lot of trips. Day trips, with my girlfriend at the time. We drove all over in my VW bug, the Cape, everywhere. We fell in love with New England in the Fall. The colorful leaves, the history, it was all so great. We ended up going into all the museums. As grad students, they were free, no admission charge.

"One of them was the Ropes. We had an experience in there. Anyway, I became a little obsessed. Spend the next year doing nothing but research on it. My girlfriend convinced me to try and make it my dissertation topic. It wasn't easy to convince the Classics department at Harvard to approve a grad student writing a book about an old house to get a doctorate. They told me to go to the school of design. But I justified it by translating a lot of newly discovered source materials I found about the place from Latin to vernacular. Anyway, here I'm, so I guess it worked."

"Let me ask you Professor, what did you find that isn't in the regular history books, like this one?" George asked, pulling out a dog-eared copy of a local Salem history book in his satchel.

"Oh, that is trash," the professor said. "Those are for tourists. They recycle a few paragraphs. You'll see, my dissertation delved into some of the unknown facts and real documents, not the urban legends. What I found was an onion."

"An onion? What do you mean?" asked George.

"What happens when you peel back an onion?" the professor asked in a Socratic tone that he probably uses in class to question his students.

"You cry?" George joked.

"Yeah, you cry, and you peel layer after layer. There is no core, no center, like an apple. Just more onion."

"Sorry, I don't get it," said George.

"Every time I found another document about the house, it led to another clue, and another document that contradicted the first. It was maddening. The thesis of my dissertation ended up being that the property was more integral to the witch trials than previously known. But I couldn't prove it. When I defended my dissertation, my colleagues grilled me for hours. I couldn't back it up. I was almost ridiculed. Fortunately, my research and translations were so detailed that they didn't question its authenticity. Just my conclusions."

"Kids call it the Madhouse, and I see you did too," George said, flipping back to the title page.

"Yeah, that's what they called it back then, too. Because of the suicides mostly, but there were other tragedies that happened to residents. It's all in there," he said, pointing at his book.

"Anyway, there's a sad footnote," said the Professor, turning away to look out the window. "You'll see it in the acknowledgements. My girlfriend died before we got engaged," he said. "I never published the book after my dissertation. Too many painful memories."

"Jesus," George said. "I'm so sorry."

"She was a grad student in this department too. Was working on a brilliant project about the Renaissance, about a guy who did some wild stuff back then. Anyway, she fell further and further behind on it. The stress got to her, I guess when she missed all her deadlines..." he said, drifting off into thought.

"Would you like to come by the house sometime, and see it again?"

"No," the professor said, without missing a beat. "Thank you, though."

"Ok, well the offer stands," George said, standing up. "Stop by anytime. I will return this in a few weeks, ok?"

"You can keep it," the professor said. "I changed my mind. Just keep it." He waved his hand.

"Thanks, you sure?"

"Yes, good luck," said the professor, turning away and clicking his computer screen back on.

RENEWAL

After they had moved in, George and Giselle had talked about redecorating. Most of the first floor was in pristine condition, but the upstairs floors and the attic had not been renovated in decades. George also toyed with the idea of building a workshop or study in the basement.

They had discussed that a fun project for Giselle would be to restore one bedroom at a time. That would give them a chance to delve into the layers of history underneath the 1960's wallpaper. But she was getting busier at the gym where her supervisor asked her to become a full-time employee, so she was losing interest in any big home renovations. George, however, was only gaining steam in planning them.

"I think I should start with the guest room, this way I won't interfere with anything, what do you think?" he asked while they ate Chinese food at the kitchen table.

"I was going to invite my mother to stay with us for Easter. Do you think that you'll be done by then?" Giselle asked.

"Definitely. That is what, months away? I plan on peeling off the wallpaper and seeing what's underneath it this weekend. Priming and painting won't take me long. The floor really needs sanding and varnishing, but that will only take me more than another weekend. There's going to be bad fumes, so we'll need to wait for a warm weekend to keep the windows open. We'll need to pick out some sconces and some accents and furniture, but your mother won't mind sleeping on a mattress on the floor, right?" he joked.

She smirked. "If your brother was coming to stay, it would need to be a king size waterbed."

"Definitely," he said. "That is actually not a bad idea," he smiled. "By the way Mel, why were you up last night?"

"Don't look at me," their daughter said, making an annoyed face. "I had my phone right next to me, I didn't even wake up to go to the bathroom."

"Come on, you were walking up and down the stairs all night. I figured your phone died and you needed a different charger or something," said George.

"Uh, no," the girl said indignantly.

"Well, if you do it again, I'm taking your phone away. You're going to be exhausted at school staying up all night," he replied.

"Mom! I didn't do *anything*! Tell Dad to stop threatening me for something I didn't do!"

"Hon, maybe you just heard noises outside again," Giselle said to George, trying to be a peacemaker.

"I don't think so, it was Sunday night, the brewery is closed," said George with his head down in his phone. "Ugh, I'm late for work again," he jumped up and grabbed his satchel. "Mike is going to kill me."

After work, he stopped at Home Depot. He was wearing a suit, but he was careful not to get it dirty or dusty. He picked up two cartons of wallpaper remover and a flat metal scraper. His plan was to spend the weekend taking it down piece by piece.

On Saturday, he woke up at seven, had few cups of coffee, grabbed his seltzer, and got right to work. He went into the guest bedroom and closed the door quietly. He mixed wallpaper remover and hot water in a bucket and used a thick paintbrush to cover a section of the wallpaper with the solution. After a few minutes, he scored the wallpaper and started to peel it back in sections.

The first strips peeled off cleanly. Underneath was a rough plaster wall that was yellowed, and water stained in parts. The second piece tore off in several sticky pieces, revealing more layers of wallpaper underneath. He had tough work ahead if that was true throughout the room.

After two hours of peeling and scraping, he had only removed a small section down to the plaster. At this rate, it would take him several more weekends to clear all four walls. He went downstairs and got another cup of coffee and came back. Soon, Giselle and Melissa would be up, so he could at least put the radio on.

As he was using the metal scraper tool to remove a section of shards, he noticed a strange marking on the wall underneath, underneath the window. It was perfectly formed and appeared to have been painted onto the plaster with black paint and an extremely fine brush.

Now this is a strange symbol, he thought to himself. Maybe it was Masonic, or maybe it was the logo of some workman who put up the plaster a long, long time ago. It reminded him of schematics for basic semiconductor circuits that he had studied in college.

He grabbed his iPhone and took several photos, with and without the flash setting. He didn't want to accidentally smudge the symbol until he could show it to Giselle, so he went back to work on a different section of the wall.

He felt woozy and opened the window to let in some fresh air. When he opened it, there was no screen on it. He suddenly felt faint and had to lean on the ledge for balance. For a second or two, the room seemed to swing from side to side. He found himself holding onto the window frame to stand up. He had almost fallen out of the window.

He sat on the floor for a minute. He just needed a quick break and a quick drink.

"Hey honey, how is it going in he—" Giselle opened the door to the guest room, bumping onto George's left foot. He was laid out flat, eyes closed and face up with his head near the window.

"George! Are you all right?!" she screamed. Powerful fumes hit her in the face. She put her hand up to her nose and ran to the window behind him to open it. It was painted shut. She banged on it to unlock it and had to push upward several times to get the frame to open. She ran to the other window. It was similarly painted closed, and she had to push it hard several times to unstick it.

She kneeled next to him. His iPhone was on the floor face down, as was his seltzer bottle. "George! Wake up!" she slapped his cheek twice.

"Hi," he said in a slurred voice. "What time is it?"

"It's late afternoon, we didn't want to bother you, what happened? Why were you painting with all the doors and windows closed?"

"What? I was using wallpaper remover, and I opened the window, I must have taken a nap or something."

"But the windows were painted shut and locked," she said.

"No, they weren't, I almost fell out of that one," he pointed to the open window which had a screen on it.

"When I came in here, they were both shut, George. Maybe you need to go to the hospital—did you hit your head on the floor?"

"—No, I'm fine," he said. "Let me go downstairs, I just need some more fresh air."

Wobbly and nauseous, he walked down the narrow stairs to the first floor and into the kitchen. It was seven o'clock in the evening.

"Wait, I was sleeping for how long?" he asked, looking at the clock on the microwave.

"Melissa and I have been shopping all day. When we left around noon, you had the radio blaring, and we didn't want to disturb you. You sounded like you were having fun. We also thought we heard you talking on your phone, you were laughing too."

"That is really weird," he said. "I never even got the radio because I didn't want to wake you guys up. And I didn't call anyone." He fished his iPhone out of his jeans pocket and looked. There were no outgoing or inbound calls.

"George, you really need to see a doctor. You might have poisoning from that paint thinner or maybe you hit your head."

"No, I'm fine, really. Just a little headache but that's just from the fumes. Oh, that reminds me. Let me show you something weird I found," he said, scrolling to the photos app. There were a series of blurry photos. The last photo's time date stamp was 9:34 a.m.

"Wait, I'm confused. I took pics of something I saw on the wall upstairs, hang on a second, let me find it," he said.

He went back up the stairs and opened the door to the guest room, which still reeked of noxious fumes even with the windows open. He looked for the spot where he had photographed the symbol. The wallpaper was firmly affixed to it. He had never removed it. He ran his hand over it and went back downstairs.

"Giselle, I'm telling you, there was a circle with weird lettering underneath. I must have accidentally let it reaffix to the wall. I just need to peel back the wallpaper again to find it—"

"—George, no," Giselle interrupted. "You need to take a break from all those fumes. It still stinks in there. Go relax and read a book outside. Give your brain some oxygen."

"Ok," he said reluctantly.

He grabbed a book and went outside.

"Here, drink some seltzer, stay hydrated," Melissa said, handing him the bottle.

"Thank you, honey," he said, as he walked outside and sat on the back porch.

HISTORY

"Are you sure you're ok?" asked Giselle in a concerned voice, as she sat on the back porch with George at dusk. "Maybe you should get an MRI, I really think maybe you hit your head."

"I really do feel fine, thanks," he said dismissively. "Those fumes were just too strong," he said. "Next time, I will make sure to open all the windows."

She looked at him skeptically.

"Really! I'm fine," he assured her.

He was getting bit by mosquitoes, so they went inside to read. He grabbed Professor Christopher's dissertation and sat in his comfortable leather chair while Giselle sat on the couch reading magazines.

Section 1: The Early Years

I have researched extensively and found evidence that the impressive gardens and what would later become the foundation of the Ropes' Mansion were maintained by Tituba, a female enslaved person owned by Samuel Parris. Parris lived nearby and has encouraged Tituba to care for the garden in addition to her household responsibilities.

The Mansion itself was later built on these grounds by Samuel Bernard in the late 1720s. Unfortunately, we know little about Samuel Bernard. He led a prosperous life in Salem Village, marrying and remarrying on four separate occasions. It is unclear what role he may have played in the Salem Witch Trials in 1692, if any.

Additionally, any connections between the Ropes Mansion itself and Tituba requires further research and examination.

He put the professor's book down and decided to go to the Salem Witch Museum the next day to learn more about the trials.

On Sundays, the museum opened at ten. He got there at 9:15 and waited until they opened so he could be guaranteed a ticket. The docent was a pretty young blonde girl dressed in Puritanical period garb. She started the tour by explaining that in January 1692, nine-year-old Betty Parris and eleven-year-old Abigail Williams, the daughter and niece of Salem Village minister Reverend Samuel Parris, suddenly went catatonic.

The volunteer continued by pointing at murals on the walls, showing images of the 1692 village. She explained that as word of the illness spread throughout Salem Village, and eventually Essex County, others began to report the same alarming symptoms. The afflicted complained that disembodied spirits were stabbing them, choking them, and jabbing them with needles and pins. Soon names were cried out as the afflicted began to identify these specters.

Tituba was the first to admit to occult practices that causes the illnesses. Suddenly, neighbors, acquaintances, and total strangers were named in the statements and examinations that followed. Gossip and stories from decades prior were dredged up as fear continued to spread. The notorious book "The Witches' Hammer" from the 15th Century was used as a handbook to interrogate victims and witnesses alike.

Over the course of 1692, she explained that 150 people across Essex County were jailed for witchcraft. Ultimately, nineteen people were hanged, and one man was crushed to death by stones after being examined by the Court of Oyer and Terminer. This was the largest witch-hunt to ever take place in America and would be the last large-scale panic to take place in the New World.

George raised his hand and asked a question. "Can you tell us more about Tituba?"

The docent seemed to have been asked this question before. "While most books about the Salem Witch Trials assumed Tituba was an African American slave, she was originally from South America, and had come to Massachusetts by way of Barbados. She was the first person to be accused by Elizabeth Parris and Abigail Williams of witchcraft. She was also the first to confess to witchcraft in Salem Village in March of 1692."

"So she was really a witch?" a young girl asked her.

The tour guide continued, "Tituba told the girls tales of voodoo and the occult. She initially denied any involvement in witchcraft, but later confessed to making a 'witch cake.'

"What is a witch cake?" asked the girl.

"In 17th century England and New England, it was believed that a witch's cake had the power to reveal whether witchcraft was afflicting a person with symptoms of illness. Such a cake or biscuit was made with rye flour and the urine of the afflicted person."

Several kids said "eww."

The docent chuckled. "The cake was then fed to a dog. If the dog exhibited the same symptoms as the ill person, the presence of witchcraft was 'proven.' Why a dog?" she asked the crowd. "Does anyone know?" Everyone shook their heads.

"Witches supposedly owned 'familiars,' which are like pets but animals that help a witch. A dog was believed to be a common familiar associated with the devil. It was then supposed to point to the witches who had afflicted the victim.

"Anyway," she continued, "Tituba confessed but that was probably due to being beaten by Samuel Parris with his intention of gaining a confession. When questioned later, she added that she knew about occult rituals from her mistress in Barbados, who had taught her. She also talked about hogs, a yellow bird, red and black rats, cats, a fox and a wolf. Tituba talked about riding sticks to different places. She even confessed that Sarah Osborne possessed a creature with the head of a woman, two legs, and wings."

"So, she *was* a witch," the girl said definitively.

"Tituba argued to Parris she was not a witch but admitted she had participated in an occult ritual when she made the witch cake to help Elizabeth Parris, so draw your own conclusions," said the guide.

"So, what happened to her?" the girl asked her.

"After the trials, Tituba remained in jail because Samuel Parris refused to pay her jail fees. In 1693, Tituba was sold to an unknown person for the price of her jail fees. We have no further record of what became of her," she concluded.

"Wow," the girl said.

"Yes, wow," said George under his breath. He walked around and took some photos of exhibits with his iPhone.

As the group of tourists were walking out the exit door to the gift shop, the volunteer handed each of them postcards that announced *Next Month: The Crucible by Arthur Miller, a play performed by the Salem High School Drama Club. Free admission with this ticket.*

"May I have two more, please?" asked George. My wife and daughter might enjoy attending with me," he said. She smiled and happily handed him several more.

TRAGEDIES

"You've got to hear this," said George to Giselle when he got home from the museum. "There is something weird about our garden."

"Yeah, I bet there's a massive amount of herbicide in there. There's no way flowers can bloom like that without weeds," said Giselle. "And you know how I hate that stuff. The previous owners probably doused it."

"Yeah," he said. "And I have never seen so many flowers bloom in August and September. I know this is a different environment than Chicago, but don't most flowers usually bloom in the spring?"

"I really don't know," said Giselle.

"Listen. I went to the witch museum this morning," he said.

"Oh, you did? I know you've been meaning to. How was it? Crowded?" she asked.

"Yeah but listen to this. Back before this house was built, a slave named Tituba planted that garden. She was the one who was scapegoated in the witch trials."

"So, they blamed her because she wasn't white. Nice," Giselle said sarcastically. "I see nothing has changed."

"Well, yeah. But here's the weird part. She confessed. To being a witch," said George.

"Of course, she did," said Giselle. "They probably tortured her. People confess to all kinds of crazy things, doesn't mean they did it. Especially poor people."

"That's true, but she apparently knew a lot about witchcraft, spells and stuff and said that she had learned it in Barbados," said George. "Let

41

me tell you what else I find odd about that garden: The shape. I have never seen an old garden laid out in a circular pattern."

"Don't all Victorian gardens look like that?" she asked.

"Not really. I mean, they are well maintained but not usually round concentric circles. Also, remember that garden was planted two centuries before the Victorian era," he said.

"Ok," said Giselle.

"Also, the size of it. Those gardens are twice the size of this house. We are talking prime real estate. Why would they have been able to own the gardens over all that time?" he asked.

"I don't know, I mean, they were rich, right? They didn't need to sell them off," she suggested.

"Yeah…" he trailed off. "Oh, by the way, next month the high school drama club is putting on the Crucible. Do you and Mel want to go with me?"

"Maybe," replied Giselle. "I will ask her."

"I'm going to go upstairs to read some more, ok?" he said.

"Sure, but don't stay up late, we have work and school in the morning," she reminded him.

He opened the professor's book to the next section.

Section 2: Four Weddings, Three Funerals

The early marriages of the Ropes Mansion are even more mysterious than the merchant who built the house.

Three of Sam Bernard's wives died of unknown causes. For example, his first wife, Mary and their infant son, died in 1720. His second wife, Rachel, died in Salem Village in 1743. Bernard remarried again to Elizabeth Williams, who died in 1753. Rumor has swirled that Bernard played some dark role in their deaths, but that has never been proven or formally alleged.

After Bernard died, the house was inexplicably vacant for at least six years. This is odd because of the house's choice location in the central village.

In 1768, Judge Nathaniel Ropes purchased the house from the nephew of Sam Bernard, who had inherited it, but refused to live in it for unknown reasons.

Ropes was a wealthy though unpopular attorney and Harvard graduate, who, despite his disrepute, held an impressive legal career.

He was a British Loyalist, which had become even more disfavorable to Salem residents after multiple tax controversies with King George. Judges had been paid by the elected representatives of the General Court, making them partial to colonial interests.

Nathaniel was therefore deemed a traitor by Salem's residents.

To save his name and reputation, he denied taking a salary from the King, yet still publicly held Loyalist views. The Salem colonists were infuriated. They viciously attacked the Ropes Mansion in March 1774, presumably to murder all its inhabitants including Nathaniel.

The Ropes Mansion was mobbed as colonists threw stones and sticks at the windows. The Colonists demanded that Ropes renounce his allegiance to the British Crown. He never had the chance, however – he died only one day after the vicious assault. He was 47 years-of-age.

His specific cause of death remains unknown. He may have had smallpox at the time of the attack although he may have been struck by a rock thrown through a window while in the house.

At the time of Nathaniel Ropes' untimely death, Salem Village was also overcome with the smallpox epidemic. The accessibility of the smallpox vaccine may have even contributed to the attack on Nathaniel Ropes: if he had been inoculated, as he could afford, he may have spread the infection to those less fortunate. That's what the mob may have thought, at least. It has been believed by his family that he was murdered on the premises.

George closed the book, drank some water, and thought to himself for a while. He fell off to sleep. The next morning, he overslept again.

"Damn," he said to Giselle as he rushed out the door. "I can't keep doing this, Mike is going to fire me."

"Mike, I'm really sorry I'm late again," said George, tossing off his suit jacket onto the back of his desk chair. "But you gotta hear this," said George. The two men were walking to their engineering firm's office kitchen in Boston.

Mike was a handsome young guy who was in his late thirties. He was always a little uncomfortable having guys like George working for him, given their age difference. However, he liked George and was willing to tolerate a fair amount of idiosyncrasy, given George's impressive experience in Chicago.

"What's this, more about your crazy house?" asked Mike, drinking coffee.

"Yeah, I don't want to tell Giselle all this stuff, she would freak out.

But listen to this," Mike said, holding the professor's book and reading from it.

> In the nineteenth century, no less than *fourteen* deaths occurred within the house, or on the grounds. Joseph Ropes had died in the house in 1818 at the age of 22. Elizabeth died at the age of 24.
>
> In 1839, Abigail Ropes met her tragic ending. Nathaniel's daughter burnt to death in her dress while in the Ropes Mansion. Her dress had ignited from the mansion's fireplace; her petticoats went up in flames.

"Holy cow," said Mike. "This is all in your new house, right?"

"Yeah," said George, flipping the pages, and continuing to read.

> In 1892, three unmarried sisters, Sarah Ropes, Mary Pickman Ropes, and Eliza Orne Ropes, inherited the house and returned to Salem from their home in Cincinnati to restore the family home, add modern plumbing and a kitchen. Nathaniel died in the house in 1893.

George looked up and said, "All three sisters were found dead in the house or on the grounds in subsequent years. Only one death (Mary's) was attributed to natural causes."

"So, that's what," said Mike, counting on his fingers, like eighteen so far?"

"More," said George. "I counted twelve mysterious deaths in the house in the 1700's, plus eighteen more in the 1800's, so we're at thirty at least by 1900."

"Didn't you buy it from the Ropes family?"

"No, in 1907, it was transferred to their Foundation, but any descendant could live in it for up to a year, and their guests were permitted to stay on premises for two weeks per year. At least until they dissolved their foundation, and it went private. I bought it from some elderly couple that bought in the nineties."

"So no like fourth cousin Ropes girls going to show up and demand free board? Too bad," joked Mike.

"Nope. Too bad." George smiled. "But wait, listen to this…" George continued reading.

> In 1928, Dorothy Ropes, a first cousin, was visiting the Mansion for a period of one month. She apparently hanged herself from the window facing the street, and her body was spotted by passersby, who alerted the authorities and informed the owners.

"Wait, is that the room you fainted in?" Mike asked.

"Yeah, well, at least I think I fainted. It was the fumes," George said and continued.

> In November 1929, only a year after Dorothy's demise, her brother Charles was briefly visiting the Mansion. He had apparently lost a fortune in the Black Friday Wall Street stock market collapse. For two days, he went missing. He was found dead in the gardens outside the Mansion from a single gunshot wound to the head. Oddly, no one had reported hearing the gun having been fired and no gun was ever recovered. However, it was deemed a suicide.

> In 1941, Edward Ropes, a one-year resident of the Mansion, was found hanged in the basement, dangling over a deep hole in the dirt, presumably of his own creation. It was believed that Edward had been drafted to fight in World War II and succumbed to despair.

Edward's brother Arthur went off to fight in the Pacific Theater and was killed in action.

In 1944, Edward and Arthur's father Charles, committed suicide by hanging in the same location as Edward, when he heard the news that Arthur had been killed.

"Oof," said Mike. "That is one bad run of bad luck. But that happened a lot back then. Rich people lost their shirts and their shit." George nodded, then looked back down at the book and kept reading.

In 1951, Eugene Ropes, Charles' son was briefly living in the Mansion while attending a nearby university. His body was found lying face down a bedroom. The coroner's report was inconclusive, but it was believed that his enlarged liver suggested alcohol poisoning as it had signs of late cirrhosis indicative of the same.

In 1953, Frances Ropes, the late Charles' Ropes daughter, died in a tragic accident. She had been visiting the Mansion and traveled to the nearby Howard Street Cemetery to visit her deceased relatives. When she was returning, witnesses reported that a late model Ford struck and killed her. However, the driver was never located.

In 1959, Frances' daughter Lois was killed while attending a nearby university when she succumbed to a fire in her dormitory room. The cause of the fire was suspected as electrical. No other victims perished in the blaze.

"Ok, so by my count, we are at 37? But not all of those died in the house. I mean, some died nearby."

"39 if you count those plus these two," George continued reading.

In 1967, Tyrell Williams, a contractor hired by the Ropes Foundation had worked in the Mansion for a period of two months to conduct extensive renovations. Bizarrely, after the Ropes Foundation paid the man for exceptional work, he retired to the basement. The caretaker presumed he was concluding his work and collecting his tools. He was found hanging later that day, from the header beam in the same location as Edward and Charles Ropes.

In 1970, the most recent death occurred prior to this writing. The Mansion's caretaker Lucy Stackhouse was found dead in the kitchen. The coroner's report concluded that she died from an overdose of barbiturates and an unknown substance.

"That's it?" asked Mike sarcastically.

"This book was written in what, 1972?" George flipped to the front page. "1974."

"You're kidding. There have been more since then?"

"I don't know. Maybe," said George. "I honestly haven't looked up newspaper records since then."

"Ok, but let's look at this like engineers. The house is what, three hundred years old?" asked Mike.

"It was built in 1720," said George.

"Yep, exactly three hundred years. Let's do the math. It has how many bedrooms?"

"Six plus the master," answered George.

"By old timey standards, that was a damn big house. Hell, that's way bigger than my house. Anyway, if we assume the average family size from 1720 to 1820 was four or five plus servants, you could have had six to seven people living in there at any given time, right?"

"Sounds about right, I guess."

"And the life expectancy was really short back then, wasn't it?" asked Mike.

"I think it was shorter than now, but not as short as people think," said George.

"Right, the infant mortality rate screws up the average. But take that out of it, you still had most people living to maybe sixty, at most, right?" asked Mike.

"I guess, what's your point?"

"I'm saying that a house that's three hundred years old has seen more than ten generations of Ropes' kids. And these were rich kids. So that meant more drinking, more partying, richer diets, and more traveling. So about forty deaths in three centuries, or about once every seven and a half years is not that crazy, is it?"

"How long have you and your family lived in Boston, Mike?"

"Let's see, I graduated from Harvard fifteen years ago. And my family has lived here since the 40's. My Dad and Mom, and their parents before that," said Mike.

"Right, so like eighty years. How many people died in your childhood house?" asked George.

"None," said Mike, "but that's only because my grandmother died in the hospital of old age. Back in the 1700's, she would have probably died at home in bed."

"Sure, but that's one. And she was in her nineties. And how many people have killed themselves in your house?"

"Touché," said Mike.

"So, one natural death might have taken place over eighty years," said George. "That sounds right."

"Ok," replied Mike. "I admit that's pretty bad. Every seven years or so, somebody is found hanging from the rafters. So, here's my theory. The Ropes kids were all screwed up. They had some bad genetic issues, alcoholism, clinical depression, maybe even schizophrenia. That runs in families, you know?"

"Maybe," said George. "But remember, not all the deaths were Ropes kids. And another weird thing are the accidents."

"Yeah, but we haven't even talked about accident statistics," said Mike. "Anyway," he said, slapping George's back, we gotta get to work, my man, but just one thing."

"Yeah?" asked George, putting the book down.

"Do we really have to have the company picnic at your place?"

DAYTIME

It was a bright, breezy Sunday morning, and Giselle had taken Melissa shopping at a mall that was located about 40 minutes away. George would have the whole day to himself. He didn't really know what to do, so he decided to take Bailey for a long walk around town.

The whole area was full of witchcraft-themed shops, stores, and museums. The Witch Dungeon Museum apparently offered reenactments and tours of a mock dungeon. The Peabody Essex Museum was a glass, modern building whose sign said it offered a pristine academic analysis. The Wax Museum and local history exhibits sported souvenir shops. Then, there was the historic Witch House offering guided and self-guided tours, as well as a variety of bookstores and shops selling all manner of occult-themed t-shirts, cauldrons, and pentagram-embossed junk. Finally, he came upon a somber memorial park that was a burial point called the Witch Trials Memorial.

When he arrived back at home after about an hour, he unleashed Bailey to run around the fenced backyard and sat down at the kitchen table. He heard a female voice speaking from somewhere inside the house and assumed that Giselle and Melissa had come home early.

"Hey guys, how was the mall?" he yelled into the living room. There was no response. "Hon?" he yelled again. No response.

He stood up and walked into the living room. He saw no one, but out of the corner of his eye, he thought he saw a wispy figure drift up the stairs.

"Hello? Giselle?" he said up the stairwell. The first thing that went through his mind was that he had inadvertently left a door open while he was walking around town. He had thought about installing a security system but hadn't gotten around to it yet. He figured that someone, probably a teenager, had decided to explore the famous 'Madhouse,' and he had caught them.

He grabbed a fireplace poker and called upstairs again. "If there is someone in this house, please come down. I will let you leave; I won't press charges, I promise. I just want you out of this house."

He heard nothing. Now, he was growing concerned. If the intruder felt trapped upstairs, they might get violent when trying to leave. Alternatively, even worse, they might feel the need to hide somewhere in a closet or something, to only depart after nightfall. That would leave the family exposed to unknown dangers.

He slowly crept up the stairs with his iPhone in hand. He was ready to dial the police if necessary. When he got to the top of the stairs, he looked around. He didn't see or hear anyone. Suddenly, he heard giggling downstairs. He knew there was no one down there. He had just been down there, and there was no way someone got into the house through a locked door or had gotten past him. He was becoming really confused.

His mind raced. Maybe someone was playing a joke on him. Could Giselle or Melissa have set up some elaborate prank on him? Could they have found a way to rig something to play sounds randomly, just to freak him out? That seemed highly unlikely. He turned and crept back downstairs and stopped halfway down the stairwell. The noises abruptly stopped.

The only noise he could hear was Bailey outside barking and looking to be let back into the locked house.

CRUCIBLE

"What's wrong, honey?" Giselle asked Melissa as she walked up to her outside Witchcraft Heights Elementary School. The girl had walked out of the school door wearing a pink backpack and sobbing.

"My new friends won't come over to play. They say our house is haunted."

"What?" asked Giselle.

"Emily and Ava, they don't want to come over. They said their parents call it the crazy house or something like that. They said it's full of ghosts."

"Oh, Mel, you know how kids are. This whole town is full of loonies, you know that."

"I know," the girl said, wiping her nose. "But I don't want to live here anymore, Mom. Maybe our house *is* haunted."

"I don't believe that, honey. I have never seen or heard a thing out of the ordinary," said her mother.

"Daddy keeps calling it the Madhouse." Giselle stopped and didn't know what to say.

"Come on, honey, let's go home and talk about it." She put her arms around her daughter and hugged her tightly.

After they walked into the back door of their house, George was sitting at the kitchen table slumped over his iPad.

"When did you get home from work?" asked Giselle.

"A little while ago, I left early."

"Ask your daughter what her friends are calling this house," she told him.

"What?" George asked Melissa.

"They're saying our house is haunted," Melissa said glumly. "They call it the Madhouse."

"Do you think it is?" he asked her. "Haunted, that is."

"I just want to have friends over. I don't want to live in a cruddy house, I want to go home," she said, frowning.

"This is our home now," he said. "And those kids are just jealous that we live in a house with history, with character," he said, justifying his decision. "Most of them probably live in McMansions."

"I don't care about character. I want a normal life," said his daughter sadly.

He shot a glance at Giselle, who crossed her arms and looked back at him with derision.

"Hey, I have an idea," he said. "I have three tickets to a play at the high school tonight. They're putting on the Crucible. It's all about Salem's history," he said.

"I don't want to learn any more about this crappy town," Melissa said, storming off into her bedroom and slamming the door.

"I guess I will go alone," he said to Giselle.

George chose to sit alone in the rear of the high school auditorium, since he wanted to take notes on his iPad without disturbing any of the families who had come to see their children perform. He had seen a performance of the Crucible off Broadway once in New York many years ago, but he remembered it only vaguely. Now that the play had new-found relevance to his residence, he would pay much closer attention. He was disappointed that Giselle and Melissa didn't want to join him.

A lanky teenage boy wearing black Puritan-style clothing walked out onto center stage. Several of his family members cheered and were hushed by others.

"Welcome, everyone. *The Crucible* is a 1953 four-act play by American playwright Arthur Miller. It is a dramatized story of the witch trials that took place here, right near where you're sitting." He gestured dramatically around the auditorium.

"While Arthur Miller wrote it as an allegory for McCarthyism, its story is largely historically accurate with only a few liberties taken for dramatic effect. It is regarded as a central work in the canon of American theater."

He walked offstage, and the red curtain was slowly lifted to reveal a dozen girls dancing around a bonfire using special effects of red light bulbs and a fan blowing tissue paper. The girls were supposed to be nude but were wearing body stockings.

A tall African American girl wearing a cloak and hood stood over the fire, holding a rubber chicken. The group was engaged in a strange pagan ritual. Reverend Parris stumbles upon the girls dancing in the forest and questions the girls' ringleader Abigail Williams who was played by a tall redheaded girl. Parris becomes convinced that Tituba's witchcraft has caused his daughter and niece to become mute and catatonic.

The girls later find out that Parris has invited Reverend John Hale, a supposed expert in witchcraft and demonology, to Salem to investigate. When Hale arrives, he has armfuls of heavy books. He comments that they are heavy with the weight of authority.

About an hour after intermission, George decides to slip out of the theater and walk home. As he does, he passes by several of the very buildings depicted in the Crucible. It's hard for him to believe that the events so dramatically depicted in the play took place in these very locations three hundred years earlier.

When he arrived at his home, his mind wandered back to Tituba. When the girls had been dancing around the bonfire and Tituba was sacrificing a chicken—that image could not have been an accident. Tituba most certainly was leading the girls in an animal sacrifice. He was determined to learn more.

The next day, he took a walk to the Salem public library, which was right on Essex Street, only few steps from their front door. He asked the research librarian if she could help him find any information about the

Ropes Mansion that might be in relatively recent historical sources such as newspapers or magazines.

She used her computer to look up a microfiche catalog. The only prominent news story was about Charles Ropes' death. George had known that in 1944, Edward and Arthur's father Charles had committed suicide by hanging in the same location as Edward, when he heard the news that Arthur had been killed.

The Salem newspaper described the incident in greater detail, explaining that Charles was only 48 when he committed suicide. Arthur had apparently been in his early twenties when he was killed during the Pacific theater of World War II. The article explained that it was odd that Arthur was shot down as no fighter planes or gunners were reported in the vicinity where his plane went down. His body was never recovered.

Charles himself had learned about Arthur's death from a grim telegram—the sort that the U.S. Navy delivered all too often during wartime.

Charles had apparently walked down to the pier immediately beforehand. In fact, several friends and other townspeople had just spoken to him to offer their condolences, and they all reported that he was eating and drinking without giving them any cause for alarm. His body was found hanging in the Ropes' basement that same afternoon.

STIRRINGS

"Honey, what are you doing now?" Giselle asked as she walked into the kitchen through the back door, putting two big bags of groceries down on the counter.

George was sitting with his legs spread on the kitchen floor. He had assembled a series of printouts of newspaper clippings, old photographs, and post-it-notes stuck onto a large piece of white posterboard.

"Hi, I'm just working on something," he muttered, while moving a piece of paper and using a glue stick on the back.

"Is this something for work?"

"Yeah no," said George.

"Is that a yes or no?" asked Giselle, confused.

"It's not for my job, but I'm doing work. Research."

"Research. Is this something to do with the house again?" sighed Giselle.

He ignored her question. He was convinced that Tituba had something to do with that garden. He had gone to Home Depot on Trader's Way and bought a lot of equipment. He had also ordered an expensive Garrett metal detector on eBay.

"I'm going to start digging up the garden," he announced.

"What?" she asked angrily. "George, if we lose that garden, I will murder you. That thing has been curated for centuries. You want to mess up those flowers? I'm not even sure they are indigenous to this area."

"I will be careful, I promise, ok? I'm just going to remove the flower beds by their roots and dig a foot or two underneath to use a metal detector. If I don't find anything, I'll just put the plants back. I might even add some fertilizer and grub control, so don't worry."

"And when are you finding time for this? I thought you were going to finish that mess you started upstairs in the guest bedroom. My mother is coming in a month, you promised it would be done."

"I'll just put something over the wallpaper I removed. She won't even notice. I will get back to that project when I'm done outside."

Giselle was starting to become concerned. There were two times when she and Melissa came home to find him sleeping on the couch, with papers and clippings and trinkets scattered all around him. The sight started to disturb Melissa, and Giselle was the one who had to clean up the mess.

In their bedroom and inside George's extra bedroom which he had converted into a makeshift study, he had pinned pictures of previous owners and newspaper clippings of their deaths on the wall, drawing lines to connect one with the other like a grand top secret police investigation.

"Giselle, come here and look at this," he said to her one evening. She walked into his study.

"What is all this?" she asked, looking around.

"I think I found a pattern," he said. "Listen to this...the guy who built this house was a merchant named Sam. Sam Bernard, ok?"

"Ok," she said, crossing her arms and listening.

"Now, Bernard wasn't originally from Salem. He came here from Deerfield. We don't know much about him. But he must have had serious dough to build this mansion right in the middle of town. He hired the best architects, buys up the prime real estate.

But his wife dies mysteriously right after this huge house is built. Then Rachel, his second wife, dies only a few years later of unknown causes. He remarries to Elizabeth, who also died of unknown causes in a couple of years later. Then, Bernard's *fourth* wife Catharine, also lived with Bernard in the mansion until his death in 1762."

"Ok, so lots of people died back then of disease, right?"

"Well, yeah but even his contemporaries thought it was strange how they were all dying off so young. Then, when he dies, his own wife moves out, leaves this valuable mansion to Bernard's nephew who refuses to even live in for almost a decade. As soon as he can, he sells it to the Ropes. You don't think that's all very strange?"

"Well, maybe he needed the money, George," she said. "And maybe she didn't want anything to do with it."

"Ok, but then wait. As soon as the Ropes move in, strange things happen. The town thinks he is a traitor. Ultimately, the owner is killed by a mob. There were so many deaths in this house or associated with this house, even Mike things it's strange."

"You told Mike about your latest obsession?" she asked. "Jesus, George. That's a great idea. Now he will think we're nuts. Why would you tell your new boss that you live in a house full of maniacs?"

"The point is, Giselle, that this house holds serious mysteries. Ever since before it was built. And they continued to the present day."

"And you're the one to solve them, right?" she asked sarcastically.

"Why not? I'm probably the first person to live here with a proper education. I can get to the bottom of this. Want to hear my theory?"

"Sure," she said.

"I think Tituba put a curse on this land. I think she was truly a witch or voodoo person or something, and I think the history books have it all wrong. I think she actually did introduce real witchcraft into this town and it made people crazy."

Giselle laughed. "Are you serious?"

"Yes, deadly serious," he said with a straight face. "I think she was exposed to witchcraft or something like that in Barbados and came here, and got people involved. She probably taught those girls real black magic. I mean, you missed the play, Giselle. Arthur Miller himself showed that Tituba was performing a pagan ritual before the girls went catatonic."

"Ok, well first that was a high school play, George. I doubt it was supposed to be accurate. But putting that aside, whatever she was doing is different from saying she *could* put a curse on the land. Maybe she knew some folk magic, you know, killing chickens for good weather or something. But that's not real, George. That's just superstition."

"Yes, of course, but how you explain the deaths that occurred here decade after decade, century after century? I mean, some of these deaths are just…bizarre. A woman's dress catching fire and burning her to death?"

"Do you hear what you're saying, George?" she asked. "You're suggesting a dead slave cursed this house three hundred years ago. Even before it was built."

He raised his eyebrow to suggest that what Giselle was saying may not be totally preposterous.

She continued. "Ok, fine. Let's assume, just for a second that you're right. Does that mean we live in a cursed house, one that *you* bought without showing me? You dragged Melissa halfway across the country to live here, and you suddenly discover it's cursed or haunted or whatever? Great," she said. "This is not the Disney Haunted Mansion, George. These are our lives; this is our *daughter's* life you're talking about."

Despite her point, he was genuinely convinced that something was deeply wrong with the home they lived in and had even started calling it the Madhouse. Giselle warned him over and over against calling it that in front of her or Melissa, but he failed at that, too.

He was overgrowing his beard, and hardly taking any showers. She started to worry if he was drinking again, but she never came across any evidence of that in the house or the trash cans.

She hoped that he would change and get it together. She tried to help him, cleaned up after him and started paying more attention to him, even tried getting him to spend more time with his daughter. For Giselle, it was like every time she thought he had moved a step forward, he moved two steps back. And it was like the house itself was feeding him with his infatuation.

He once ran up to her in the kitchen, all excited, and she was glad to see him looking a bit different; much livelier. She was expecting some sort of growth and maturity, but her hopes were quickly dashed when he brought out yet another set of old news clippings, saying that there were, in fact, messages hidden in pictures and throughout Salem itself.

George was becoming convinced that Giselle herself wasn't enlightened, that she was stuck in the loop; that she was a puppet, and he was going to be the one to uncover the strings behind this house.

He had started to notice that Melissa had started to avoid him, and acted as though she feared him, but he didn't blame her. He was convinced that they would all see that he was right when he finally unmasked the true workings. He wasn't going to stop until then. It was the most important thing to him right now, to end the mystery of the dark history of the Ropes Mansion. He was convinced that he and his family were going to end up dead as well, just like all the previous owners, unless he did something about it.

YANKEES

"You can't seriously be wearing a Cubs jersey to a Yankees Sox game, George," joked Mike as the men sat behind third base.

"Damn right," said George. "Cubbies all the way, baby!"

"Ok, ok. Throw the guy a bone," said Frank, an African American heart surgeon who was friends with Mike since their days at Harvard. "The Cubs are the only team more pathetic than the Sox."

"Blasphemy," Mike said.

"How did you get these sweet seats, Mike?" asked George.

"The firm has season tickets to home games at Fenway Park for as far back as anyone can remember," he explained. "Milton bought them a million years ago and started a lottery so you can put in to request the Yanks tickets. This time, I came out on top," he said as he cheered the Red Sox pitcher for striking out the top of the Yankees batting order.

"Last year, I got squat. George, how is it going on the Friedman project?"

George gulped. "I haven't really had time to finish that project. I plan to reach out to Mr. Friedman soon and get some input on the con-figurations, but I haven't had time to do that yet. It will get done this week; I promise."

"Ok," said Mike. "It better get done, or Charlie will come down on me. And if he comes down on me, you know what that means..." He didn't need to say it. George knew that if he fell too far behind on the project, Mike couldn't cut him any more slack. Fortunately, Mike changed the subject.

"Tell Frank about your haunted house," joked Mike, sipping a beer.

"Haunted house? Uh oh," said Frank, passing an Italian sausage hero from the vendor down the row.

"I think it's cursed. Honestly," said George.

"Cursed? Uh oh," said Frank again. "My last house felt cursed because my neighbors sucked. They bought a pit bull and let it run around my yard without a leash. I wanted to kill that dog," he chuckled. "Then the neighbor's wife starts planting bamboo. Bamboo. Like, what are we doing, feeding a panda bear? You know how hard it is to remove bamboo? It spreads like wildfire."

"Not that kind of cursed," George said. "You ever been to Salem?"

"The witchy town?" asked Frank.

"Yeah, near Danvers."

"Oh, I know where it is. I grew up in Ashland and my wife's from Natick. We used to go there for kickass Halloween parties. Best one is at the Hawthorne Hotel. Open bar all night. Damn, good deal," said Frank, giving Mike a high five. "You should check it out. Good times."

"George doesn't drink anymore," said Mike sullenly.

"Is that right?" asked Frank.

"Yeah, not anymore," said George, sipping on seltzer he had brought with him.

"And you from Chicago? Damn, you must've partied hearty back in the day."

"No doubt," said George. "That's all behind me now."

"Wait, so tell me more about your Beetlejuice house. You singing the banana boat song when your wife is serving dinner or something?" asked Frank. "What was her name, Winona Ryder?" The men laughed.

"Nothing like that. There've been a ton of deaths in the house. Accidents, suicides, even murders."

"No kidding," said Frank. "Murders?"

"Way back anyway. A mob caught the owner taking bribes from the Redcoats during the Revolutionary War. Killed him on the spot. Other deaths were suspicious too. Suicides, a whole lot of them. Recently, too."

"Jesus, hardcore," said Frank. "That's atrocious."

"Yeah, we tried to figure out if the house had an unusual number of deaths, given its size and age," said Mike. "We ended up with a death every seven and a half years."

"Yikes. That's bad. George, you ever…see or hear stuff at night?" asked Frank.

"I'm not sure," said George. "Nothing specific, but it's just a really weird house."

"What does Giselle think?" Mike asked.

"Is that your wife?" asked Frank.

"Yeah. She's not thrilled, let's put it that way," replied George. "I may have bought the house without telling her, and I also may have bought it without knowing its history."

"Damn, dude. My wife would murder my ass if I put her in a haunted house," joked Frank. "She'd move us out in a weekend. No questions asked."

"Yeah, it's getting that way," said George. "I feel like if I can just figure out the history, maybe it's something we can get past. I feel like there's some mystery to this curse that I can figure out, you know?"

"No, I don't really know, man," said Mike. "But I'll take your word for it. Hey, hand me that popcorn."

"Hey, I just thought of something," said Frank. "Let's say you did find out something bad about the house, like it really is the poltergeist house or whatever. Don't you got to reveal it? Like I heard that somebody who bragged they had a haunted house to Reader's Digest or something, and then when they went to sell it, they didn't disclose it. Years later, the buyers sued them, saying they were being kept up all night by chains rattling, real Scrooge stuff. Anyway, I heard the Judge said they couldn't deny it was haunted."

"I guess I haven't worried so much about the resale price," George said. "And in this market, people are so hard up for houses, they'd buy the Amityville house and put in a hot tub." The men laughed.

"The real problem," George continued, "is that I feel like something is just…wrong. I can't explain it. I just constantly feel like I'm being watched. Like there is a presence in the corners. I have heard voices, even seen things. It's just bizarre."

"Yeesh," said Frank. "I dunno man, I don't think I could live like that. After a 16-hour shift at the hospital when I get home, I just want to soak in my own little jacuzzi. Last thing I need are little ghost eyes starin' at me, ya know?" he laughed.

"Yeah, I hear you," said George. "I'm starting to wonder if I made a big mistake buying it."

"Ah, don't think that way," said Mike. "You'll get used to it eventually. By the way, tell us more about that hot girl at the brewery."

"Hot girl at a brewery?" asked Frank. Now you're talking my language. Do tell."

"Oh, Marlena. Yeah, she owns the brewery next door to me," said George.

"I haven't seen her yet," said Mike, but to hear George describe her, oof. That's probably why he isn't getting the Friedman project done," he nudged George jokingly.

"Wait," said Frank, "you're on the wagon, you're married, you bought a haunted house next to a brewery with a hot girl working there and you're a Cubs fan?"

"Yeah, I guess so," said George, smiling.

"Man, we gotta hang out more often. Mike, you have some crazy ass friends!"

GARDENS

It was a tepid summer morning, and George got up early. He had terrible stomach cramps during the early morning hours, so he figured he would just wake up and get the day started. He went outside to the garden and used a spade to cut around the first section of flowers closest to the house. He had to use a cultivator to loosen it. Once he was able to remove the flower bed, he gingerly placed it in a wheelbarrow.

The soil underneath was visible. It was dense and a sandy loam. He got the metal detector and set it to a sensitive setting that could probe down at least a foot and a half underneath the surface. He also set it so that it would not ignore any metallic objects, no matter how small.

He got no readings. He took his shovel and dug down deeper. He figured that the further he went, the deeper the metal detector could sense. He found nothing but a few small rocks.

He added loose fertilizer and grub control, carefully replaced the loose soil back into the hole, placed the flower bed back on top and marked it with a small yellow flag.

He moved onto the second and third sections and did the same thing. Three sections had taken him two hours, because he wanted to be sure that he didn't disturb the flower beds, as Giselle had warned him.

But he was growing frustrated. He had not found a single object, not even a bottle cap. He was also getting hot and tired. By the time he reached the fifth section, he was getting sloppy and just throwing the flowers aside.

Finally, the metal detector buzzed and beeped when he placed its coil over the deep hole. He waved it back and forth. It buzzed again.

He laid it down and waved a small orange wand that looked like a flashlight to pinpoint the source. There was a faint beep, so he got the large shovel to dig deeper. As he did, he heard a metallic sound as he struck something hard. It wasn't a rock.

He used the smaller shovel to dig even deeper. He saw the rounded top of a small pewter tarnished metallic box laying upright. He pried it up out of the soil. The box was in the shape of a tapered hexagon and reminded George of the shape of an old-style coffin. He saw no hinges but was completely sealed with black wax around the seams.

He wiped his sweaty brow and stood up with the box to brush the pewter off in the sunlight. Given the depth of this item underneath the flower bed, the item was clearly underneath the ground for a long time.

Excited with his find, he took it into the kitchen. Giselle and Melissa were sleeping late this morning. He laid a hand towel down on the table and got a pair of sharp Henckels scissors. He hacked away at the black wax. It was hard but chipped away in chunks. When he reached the seam underneath, he put the point of the scissor inside and pried the box open.

Inside was a tiny, tarnished cross. It was undecorated. There were also two small bones. They were dark yellow and looked to be from a medium sized mammal or large bird. He could not tell if they were femurs or tibia.

At the bottom of the box was a yellowed card that had partially rotted on its corners. It had a handwritten image inscribed on it in black ink. The symbols on the top and bottom looked vaguely Masonic, and the coffins resembled the shape of the box itself. George was so excited that he had to wake Giselle up.

"Honey, look at what I found! Come downstairs!"

She was groggy. "What? What's wrong?"

"Come look at what I found in the garden."

"Can you give me a few minutes to go to the bathroom and get changed at least?" she asked. "This is supposed to be the one day I can sleep late," she said, clearly annoyed at him.

"Ok but hurry up!" he said enthusiastically.

When she slowly made her way downstairs wearing a bathrobe, George was frantically searching on his iPhone to identify the drawing on the card.

"I didn't even get dressed yet. What did you find, George?" she asked.

"A box in the garden, look."

She looked at the kitchen table and saw the animal bones, cross and card and the open box.

"Where did you find that?" she asked.

"Outside in the dirt."

She looked out the kitchen window and saw the mess he had made outside.

"George! You promised me that you wouldn't destroy the flowers!"

"I know, I will fix that, but look!" He showed her the card.

"What is that?" she asked, annoyed.

"I don't know, I'm trying to figure it out."

"Maybe some kid put it there. This place is the Halloween hotspot, after all," she said, pouring some coffee.

"I don't think so. It was buried pretty deep, and it looks pretty old."

"What does it mean?" she asked as she absentmindedly refilled the coffee maker.

"I don't know, I have been searching it. It looks like it might be either Masonic or voodoo or occult or something," he said, holding his iPhone.

"What are those little bones?" she asked.

"I don't know. Maybe an animal?" he said.

"My guess is that it's a dead pet's grave," she suggested.

"Maybe," he said. "But there are only two bones."

"Yeah, but maybe that's all that's left. You said yourself it's old. Maybe it decomposed. My guess is that it was some poor kid's parakeet."

"But what about the symbol?" he asked.

"Good luck? I mean there's a cross in there, right?"

"Yeah, but I think it's something stranger than that," he said.

"Ok, well, I'm taking Giselle to a birthday party this afternoon over in South Peabody, so please clean this up, and fix the garden, ok? You promised."

"Ok," he said, looking down closely at the box. "By the way," said George. "Melissa was at it again. I didn't want to wake you up, but she was wandering around the whole night. I think she was on her iPhone with someone because I heard her giggling."

"I didn't hear anything, but I was exhausted. I will lecture her later," she said.

"I think we may need to put in a security system," said George. "We don't need her wandering out of here late at night."

"That's a good idea, just something simple on the doors. Don't put on your engineering hat and install something crazy, ok?" she said.

"Yeah, I will look into it," said George, staring down at the box.

DISRUPTION

"What the—" said George, interrupting himself. The next morning, he had walked outside and found the white fence near the front of their house knocked down in three sections. The house's side window had been broken, although he hadn't heard it happen. Nothing seemed stolen, and the hole in the glass was not large enough for someone to get through. But had someone wanted, they could have unlatched the window and shimmied through, opening the back or front doors and burglarized their home.

There were empty plastic beer cups on the ground that bore the Madhouse Brewery's logo on them. Part of the house had weird graffiti written on it with a black marker.

He stormed back into the house. "Giselle!" he shouted.

"I'm in here," she said, folding laundry.

"These damn kids knocked our fence down and broke a window!" he yelled, showing her the stack of empty beer cups. "They even wrote something on the house."

"You're the one who wanted to live here," she said. "And please don't swear.

"They get drunk almost every night and constantly make a mess out there. I personally think that brewery is serving underage kids," he said.

"I don't know," she said, "but we need a good security system, you said so yourself."

"Yeah, I also need to get that window fixed and get the graffiti off the house," he said.

After ordering a replacement windowpane, he drove to an electronics store about twenty minutes away. They specialized in all kinds of do-it-yourself security systems. They had professional touch screen panel command centers, night vision video cameras, window sensors, motion lights, automated telephone dialers, even remote-control key fobs. Despite Giselle's request, he spent over two thousand dollars, buying all their top-of-the-line equipment. He came home and started wiring it up.

He mounted video cameras in virtually every room. He put motion sensors at the top and bottom of the stairwell, and window break sensors on every window on the first floor. No one was getting in or out of this house without him knowing it.

Melissa walked into the dining room and saw him on the ladder. "What is this?" she asked skeptically.

"This is your new babysitter," he said, screwing in a motion sensor on the ceiling. "If you keep wandering around at night, I will know about it, and so will the eye in the sky." He pointed to a video camera that had night vision LED's all around its lens.

"And only Mom and I will know the PIN. So, if you ever decide to go outside, the whole neighborhood and the local police precinct will know."

"Mom! Why is Dad putting us in prison?!" she screamed. "I'm not walking around at night, stop saying that!"

Giselle walked into the dining room. "Honey, it's for our own good," she said. "Someone broke our window and fence last night. We live in a city; we can't have people breaking in or worse."

Melissa stormed off in a huff.

"George, don't you think this is a little much?" Giselle asked, fiddling with a video camera that was laying on the dining room table.

"Nope," he said. "We need to be safe."

He set up video cameras and equipment all over the house, watching and recording every corner, recording time lapse videos, and permitting remote playback on his iPhone.

That night after everyone went to sleep, he remotely armed the system and went to bed. In the middle of the night, he woke up when he heard a cracking sound inside the house. He suspected that whoever had broken the window and the fence may have come back to break into the house. He was almost excited to catch someone in the act.

He had set up the application on his iPad that would allow him to look at any one of the cameras at any time. He grabbed it off the nightstand, turned it on and clicked on the app. The indoor cameras were all in night vision mode.

He saw nothing on any of them and none of the motion sensors had been tripped. Nothing was moving inside the house. But he swore that he could hear loud footsteps on the staircase. He waited and stared at the cameras. Nothing. He got up slowly and creeped over to the bedroom door. He opened it and looked out. He saw nothing. The sounds abruptly stopped.

He thought maybe he didn't have the cameras positioned correctly and Melissa was sneaking out of her room to test him. He walked over to her bedroom and slowly opened her door. She was sound asleep in bed, quietly snoring. There was no way she could have walked past him after making any sounds on the stairs.

He went down the hall and looked up at the stairwell cameras. They seemed to be working properly. He went back into his bedroom and grabbed his iPad and hit rewind. He saw himself walking and looking up at the cameras. Everything was working perfectly. He decided to go back to sleep and investigate further in the morning.

He spent over two hours checking every connection, every wire and every outlet. Everything seemed to be working fine. He could not explain or account for the noises that he had heard the night before. While he strongly suspected the girl had found a way to dodge the cameras and his view the night before, he didn't dare confront Melissa about her wandering the house again, as he had no evidence. He went back to sleep.

At exactly 3:15 a.m., a deafening screech blasted throughout the Ropes Mansion and could be heard all the way down the street at the museum. George thought he was having another nightmare, but Giselle woke up too.

SMOKE

Within minutes, a blazing red fire truck pulled up in front of 318 Essex Street. On its side was stenciled in gold lettering "When Summoned, We Obey," an odd slogan associated with the Salem Fire Department. Its headquarters was located at 48 Lafayette Street, which was less than two blocks away. Consequently, it took longer for the truck to pull out of its driveway than to arrive at the Ropes house.

"We received an automated fire alarm signal, sir," said Alan Thomas, the Fire Chief as the fire truck pulled up in front of the house. "Everyone ok?"

"Yes, yes, thank you," said George.

"Anyone else inside? Pets?"

"No, we have the dog, no one else in there," said Giselle.

"Ok, we'll need to inspect the entire building, top to bottom," said the fire chief.

"Ok, no problem," said George, standing at the doorway to the house with Melissa and Giselle and Bailey at his side. "I just installed this system yesterday," George said. "But I'm sure that it wasn't a false alarm because I smelled smoke right after the alarm went off. Once my wife and daughter were outside, I went back in and looked around. I didn't smell it again and didn't see anything."

"Never a good idea, sir," said the Chief. "Let us do what the Commonwealth pays us for," he said, signaling to four firemen to enter the house and inspect, starting in the attic.

"Please step outside and away from the house, ladies," he said to Giselle and Melissa.

"My guess is a small electrical fire somewhere, maybe in the walls," said the Chief to George. "That might explain why you smelled smoke and then it seemed to dissipate."

"Maybe," said George. "But it didn't smell like an electrical fire, I'm an engineer, I know what burning plastic smells like when a wire shorts. This was stronger, like the smell of burning charcoal or even church incense, if that makes any sense. The sensor triggered was in the basement, by the way."

"Textiles can give off strange smells when they burn. In any event, we'll be thorough and check the attic to the basement, so please be patient."

By now, a second fire truck and ambulance had pulled up outside the house. "I, uh, didn't make a distinction between a fire alarm or a burglar alarm when I installed the autodialer," he whispered to Giselle. "So, they may send the National Guard."

Just as he said that, three police squad cars pulled up behind the other rescue vehicles.

They greeted George and the Fire Chief along with the EMT's. "We received an urgent automated emergency message at the precinct," said the police officer.

"So did we," said an EMT, emerging from the ambulance's passenger door.

"Uh, yeah, I smelled smoke and I guess a detector picked it up," said George, a little embarrassed by the massive show of force he had called upon.

"Ok well, was anyone affected by smoke inhalation? Maybe you need some oxygen?" asked the EMT.

"No, no, it was just a pungent scent. We didn't see anything. In fact, only I smelled it."

"Yeah, I didn't smell anything," interrupted Giselle.

"Me neither, Dad," piped up Melissa.

"Ok, that's good. But a brand-new smoke detector picked it up, so that means I wasn't imagining it," said George.

A tall firefighter carrying an axe walked outside to the Chief.

"Can I have a word with you a minute, boss?" he whispered. The Chief stepped aside with him.

They both came back a few minutes later.

"Sir, can we ask you a question about your basement?" asked the Chief.

"Sure, what is it?"

"We went down there, and there was definitely a very strong smell of something burning, it smelled like church incense or something like that. But it seemed to only be on the side of the basement near the new interior wall. Any idea what's behind it?"

"No, sir," said George. "I don't think it's a load bearing wall. I noticed it when we moved in. It's out of place, not connected to the foundation from what I can tell"

"Could have an old electrical panel behind the wall that burnt out," said the fireman. "But we checked the electrical main, and she looks fine."

"This house is ooooold," interrupted another young fireman. "Could be an old electrical line coming in that fried back there. Might need to break it down."

"Break it down? What do you mean?" asked George.

By now, a small crowd of neighbors had become interested onlookers, despite it being nearly four o'clock in the morning.

"If we have a smoldering fire in a location that is inaccessible," said the chief, "like behind a retaining wall or something like that, we might have to break it down. We can't just leave a house smoldering just because the fire isn't visible."

"Wait, so you want to tear down my basement wall?" George asked.

"We might have to," said one of the firemen. "Otherwise, if we leave and poof, there goes your house. You could be dead by morning. And that's on us."

"That's some hard cement down there," said George.

"We could try the axes, and if that didn't work, we have a jackhammer at the station. Wouldn't take us 20 minutes to tear that whole wall down. Now, if it's load bearing, you could have a problem. This house is an architectural gem. I don't want the City of Salem breathing down my neck because we destroyed a historical artifact if we didn't need to."

"I tell you what," suggested George. "Even if it's a load bearing wall, which I doubt, drill a hole in it, and put a flashlight through it or something. I can construct a temporary header and secure a brace across it, in case. Worst case, I can add a couple of jacks and get the header supported with sill plates later. If smoke comes out of your hole, well then we know you gotta tear it down. If nothing, then maybe I can patch it up and decide whether to leave the jacks or remove them."

"You're an engineer, right?" asked the Chief.

"Yep," answered George.

"Ok, it's your house. You guys check out the rest of the place?" asked the Chief.

"Yep, boss. The detector that picked it up was in the basement, which is weird, because he said he smelled it on the second floor."

"Ok, well, guys, get to work," said the Chief.

HAMMERS

S oon, the quiet moonlit night of Essex Street was broken by the unmistakable din of a jackhammer underneath the earth pounding away at an old basement wall.

"This isn't original," said George to the Fire Chief, picking up a pinch of the silty stones that had accumulated on the ground near where a jackhammer was trying to punch a hole. "This is called natural cement—Rosendale—very rare. Typically comes from a small region in the mountains. It's strange to find it here."

"It's hard as hell," said the fireman, chipping away at it. "We don't use this hammer much, but it just ain't getting through."

"How could smoke have gotten through?" asked George.

"Damned if I know," said the Chief, as they stood in the basement. "My guess is that there's something smoldering back there and pressure built up from the smoke. It made its way into the heating ducts or plumbing system. Who knows? Most important thing is that we caught it. If you hadn't, oof. Whole place might have gone up."

"Yeah," George nodded, looking back at the firemen working at destroying a portion of the old wall piece by piece.

"Got it!" said the fireman, as a fistful sized chunk of cement pushed through. "Holy cow, this thing is 10 inches thick in parts!" he put his arm through the hole, and it almost reached his elbow.

"Any heat?" asked the Chief.

"Let me see," he put his MagLite flashlight in and shone it around. A bit of smoke was visible in the light beam.

"Smell that?" asked the Chief.

"That is exactly what I smelled," said George.

"Get the eye," yelled one fireman to another.

"Shhh, wait a second…" interrupted a fireman.

Everyone went silent for a minute. There was a strange sound like a cat in pain, mewing repeatedly.

"You got a cat?" asked the fireman.

"No—" said George. "A dog, but he's outside with my wife."

"Shh—" interrupted the Chief. "I heard it again."

Silence. Then nothing. They each looked at each other.

Another fireman pulled out a device that had a long snakelike neck with a lens. He hooked it up to a small LCD color monitor and pushed the tube through the hole. He then took a powerful floodlight and pitched it into the room behind the wall.

"What the—?" said the fireman, as he moved the eye around. "Hit record, Ethan," he said to another fireman who was operating the monitor.

Five men, including the Chief and George huddled around the small monitor to peer beyond the wall.

From what they could see, there was nothing electrical visible. There was no coaxial cable, no Romex, no wiring, no fuse panels, absolutely nothing. The room consisted of a fifteen-foot by fifteen-foot empty space. However, they immediately noticed several oddities.

First, in the center of the floor was a small pile of fine ash. Wafts of smoke were visible wafting up from it, as though it had gone out only a few hours ago.

The second was a white chalk circle apparently drawn on the floor. It looked about nine feet in diameter and glowed in the light from the floodlight. Symbols were drawn crudely inside the perimeter, but they didn't appear to be English characters or letters.

Finally, the far side of the basement which formed the western foundation wall made the men gasp. A heap of yellowed bones was strewn on the floor in the corner. From the shape and size of the ribs and femurs strewn around it, it was clearly human skeletal remains.

A skull that was missing teeth lying on its side on the eastern side of the room, at least ten to fifteen feet away from the rest of the body. Next to the skull were several large rectangular books.

"Holy shit," said the fireman, dropping the snakelike camera. "Is that--?"

"Sure looks like it," said the Chief. "Go get the dicks."

"Dicks?" asked the fireman.

"Uh, the cops…the guys upstairs in blue uniforms. Get them before they jet. This is now a crime scene."

"Oh, right," said the young fireman.

Two men, one dressed in a police uniform walked down the basement stairs toward the group of men who were huddled around the glowing LCD monitor.

"Bruce, check it out," said the Chief.

The uniformed officer walked over and leaned in to look at the screen.

"You boys just open that up?" he asked the police officer.

"Yep," Ethan said. "That's what greeted us. Smoke detector had gone off," he said, pointing at the sensor mounted above them on the ceiling rafter. "We broke into it, room was sealed shut. Weird thing is there's smoke coming off the ashes," he said, pointing into the room.

The other cop leaned in and investigated the hole with a flashlight.

"Ok, so let me get this straight," he said to George. "You smelled smoke and called this in?"

"Yeah, well this smoke detector picked it up, the alarm system called it in, but yes, I smelled it too. Upstairs," he gestured.

"Chief, any imminent threats?" asked the police officer.

"I don't think so," said the Fire Chief.

The police officer took out a yellow roll of tape out of a duffel bag and taped it across the hole.

A detective in plainclothes had been listening and had walked halfway down the stair to the basement.

"Let's go back up," the detective said. He turned around and walked back up.

George accompanied the detective, police officer and the Fire Chief up to the Master Bedroom.

"Hi, I am Detective Massimo, Tony Massimo. Just call me Tony. So where exactly were you?"

"Right here, in bed, sleeping," said George, pointing into the master bedroom.

"You got a problem with burglars?" asked the uniformed cop, noting the presence of several motion sensors and night vision cameras on the stairwell.

"Well, we had a window broken last night. Nothing taken, but we just moved in, so I just installed it today."

"Today?" the detective asked, surprised.

"Yes," I just wired it up.

"I see," said the detective. "Mind if we look around a bit?"

"No, of course not, go ahead," replied George.

"Oh, and please get your wife and kids over here, I will need to talk to them, too."

"Sure, it's my wife and daughter, that's it." George went out to get them.

The uniformed officer and the detective wandered the hallway of the upstairs together. They peeked into the rooms that were still filled with boxes. They noticed that one of the rooms had some of the wallpaper peeled off.

"Detective, this is my wife Giselle, and our daughter Melissa."

"Nice to meet you, I'm Detective Tony Massimo. Just call me Tony."

"Detective? I thought we had a fire. Is there a problem?"

"That's what we are trying to figure out, ma'am," said the other detective, who had not introduced himself.

"Just tell us exactly what happened, in your own words," said the uniformed officer.

Giselle said shakingly, "Nothing, I mean, George's new security system woke us up from a sound sleep, it was about three a.m. He grabbed my shoulder and told me to wake up and get Melissa that he smelled smoke and the alarm was blaring. I ran to get her, and we ran downstairs to the front door. That's it."

"And where was your husband?"

"I think he went back inside and said he was looking around to see what was going on. Then the firemen pulled up. That's it. Can I ask what is going on?"

The two officers looked at each other. "Ma'am, can we speak in private with you and your husband?" They glanced over at Melissa.

"Uh sure," Giselle said. "Mel, just wait here."

George and Giselle walked into the kitchen with the police and fire chief.

"The fireman just found a body in your basement," said the detective. Looks like it's been there awhile but we don't know for how long. But there were smoldering ashes behind a seemingly bricked up wall. We are trying to figure it all out."

"A what?" asked Giselle, stunned.

"A skeleton," whispered George.

"I need to sit down," said Giselle, losing her footing.

The detective grabbed a chair and sat her down in it before she could lose her balance.

"You found a dead body, in my house?" asked Giselle, putting her elbows on the kitchen table. "What am I supposed to think? With the way George has been acting lately and this house, I can't say I'm surprised."

The detective shot the uniformed cop a glance.

ASHES

"George, are we telling Melissa about this?" asked Giselle, covering her mouth and sitting at the kitchen table. The girl was still outside the front door of the house and did not yet know what was going on.

"May I suggest telling her the truth, ma'am?" asked the uniformed police officer, leaning into the couple's conversation. "My own daughter is 11, and my wife and I realized that they're smarter than we are. They'll figure it out on their own, and then they won't trust us if we lie. Just my two cents."

"I think he's right. I think we need to tell her," said Giselle, looking back at George.

"Ok, let's bring her in here," he said, agreeing.

The police officer nodded and went outside to usher the girl into the kitchen.

"Mom, Dad, what's wrong?" Melissa asked, looking nervously around the kitchen at the police and her parents.

"Mel," George said, "Remember when I smelled smoke earlier? Well, we still can't figure out what caused a fire in the basement behind an old wall, but when the firefighters opened it up, they found something strange."

"What?" she asked nervously.

"A skeleton," said Giselle, still covering her mouth.

"A what?" asked Melissa again.

"A body," said George. "The police are going to take it out of here and investigate it."

"Oh...my...God. There was a rotting corpse in our house, while we all slept and ate here? All this time?" She looked completely horrified.

"Yeah," said George. "And we were lucky they found it."

"Lucky?" said Melissa. "What is lucky about finding a dead body in your basement?" she asked.

"Well, we can make sure it gets buried properly," said Giselle, still trying to process the incident in her mind.

The detective spoke. "Listen, guys, I have to keep your whole basement sealed off. Is that ok?"

"Yeah," George said. "Giselle, is that ok with you?"

"Yeah, the laundry room is up here, and the heat won't go on for a few months, so yeah."

"Ma'am, may I ask you a couple more questions privately?" asked the detective.

"Me?" asked Giselle, pointing to herself.

"Yes," said the detective matter-of-factly.

"Sure," she said, standing up to follow him into the dining room. George shot them a nervous glance.

"What's wrong, Detective?" she asked.

"You said earlier that your husband had been acting strange lately?" he whispered.

"George?" she asked.

He nodded. "Yeah, anything we should know about?"

"No, I don't think so. I mean, let me think for a minute. Why? Why are you asking?"

"Whenever there's a homicide or accidental death or whatever this is, we need to close the loose ends. We are going to have forensics in Boston try to identify the body from dental records and DNA. It might be a missing person, we don't really know yet.

"But we still can't figure out what or who caused the fire behind that wall that led us to the body. Your husband was the last person in the house, and we can't really square how he smelled the smoke from the basement on the second floor, when you guys didn't. So we were just wondering if he had been up to anything strange lately, that's all."

"Other than the fact he bought this house without telling me?" she scoffed.

"He did?"

"Yeah, we were living outside of Chicago. He came here to visit on a business trip and fell in love with this place," she said, looking around at the room. "First time I saw it was the day we moved in."

"Did he say why he wanted to buy it?"

"No, he said he fell in love with it at an open house, that's it."

"Anything else?"

"A few weeks ago, he wanted to remove some old wallpaper in the guest room upstairs."

"Oh, right," he said. "Top of the stairs, left?" he gestured.

"Right. He was in there all day, breathing in those fumes, the paint thinner fumes. And when we went in there, he had fainted."

"Fainted?" asked the detective, looking up from his notebook. "Like passed out? Unconscious?"

"Yeah, she said," whispering. "I was worried about him, I thought maybe he hit his head on the floor, but he refused to get an MRI. Then there was the garden…"

"Garden?" asked the detective, looking up again from his note pad.

"Yeah, George has been digging it up, looking for clues or something—but why is any of this relevant, Detective?"

"Clues? Like I said, I just need to close the loop. I will speak to you guys once we get back the lab report on the body. Like I said, might be a missing person or something like that. But we'll see."

"One last thing," he said.

"Yes?" asked Giselle.

"You might want to keep this quiet. We don't know whose body that is, and the local news is going to be all over this."

Three news crews from Boston were already at the house by the time they returned home.

White double-parked vans were stenciled with loud lettering that said NBC10 Boston, as well as New England Cable News.

"What the hell is this?" George said, as he pulled up. "How could the news have broken already?"

"Must be a leak in the Salem P.D.," Giselle said.

"Ma'am?" A young woman stood at their car door, as Giselle got out. "Yes?"

"Is it true that the dead body of a murdered witch was walled up in your basement?" she asked, holding up a large microphone that said 7 News Boston.

"Who said it was a murdered witch?" asked Giselle, dumbfounded by the question.

"So, you *did* find a body?" asked the excited reporter while a cameraman stood behind her, pointing a large video camera at Giselle.

George walked up behind her and said, "Thank you, now please get off our property," closing the car door and pulling Giselle away from the conversation and toward their front door.

"Oops," said Giselle. "I didn't mean to talk to them."

"Remember what Detective Tony said? Let's keep this quiet," he said, as they closed the front door behind them.

"Sure," Giselle said. "Story of the year and it's in our basement. Let's keep it quiet," she said, jokingly making the sign of zippering her mouth closed. They both laughed for the first time in a while.

"I know, but we don't know much, so let's just wait," George said.

When Giselle walked to their car the next morning to bring Melissa to school, the Boston news crews had been replaced with local reporters who were holding note pads.

"No comment," smiled Giselle.

"I'm a reporter with the Salem Access News," said a middle-aged woman. "Can you give me an exclusive quote?"

"Sure, how about 'we love Salem'?"

"That's it?" asked the reporter, writing it down anyway.

"Yep, for now," smiled Giselle, helping Melissa into the car.

EVIDENCE

"What does this mean?" George asked the young volunteer at the Witch Museum whose tour he had attended a few weeks ago. He had sneaked out the side entrance of their house to avoid the reporters who were still mingling around the sidewalk several days after the news had broken.

"What is it?" the girl asked, picking up the plastic baggie and staring at the scrap of paper George had found in the garden.

"I found it in my garden...at the Ropes house," he said.

As soon as she heard mention of the Ropes house, she looked at him nervously. "Uh, I have no idea, but let me get my supervisor over here... Sasha? Can you please talk to this gentleman?"

A middle-aged woman with dyed blonde hair wearing a pants suit came over. "He's from the Ropes house," whispered the docent, handing him back the baggie.

"Yes, may I help you?" the woman asked cautiously. Her name tag said "Sasha, Director of Salem Witch Museum."

"I sure hope so," he said. "We moved into the Ropes Mansion last October, and I have been doing a lot of research on the history of the house."

"Are you...George Lawson?" she asked.

"Yes, yes I'm. Have we met?"

"No, she said. I heard about you on TV. We heard about...the body in your basement."

"Yes, terrible thing," he said. "We are still waiting for the dental records and DNA testing to come back from the police lab."

"Incredible story," she said. "Salem sure keeps its secrets, doesn't it?"

"Yes. In fact, the reason I'm here is that I stumbled on this while digging in our garden." He handed the plastic baggie up to the Director. "Can we keep this quiet?"

"Sure. That's ok," she said, putting her hand up. "I don't need to touch it. You said you found it where?"

"In my garden."

"Was it inside anything, or was it just lying on the ground?" she asked.

"It was inside a pewter box. With some bones and a cross," he said. "It was buried about two feet down."

"I see," she said. "And you say that you stumbled on it? Two feet down?" She looked at him skeptically over her wire rimmed glasses.

"Well, I was digging in my garden. Anyway, what is it?"

"It's called a veve," she said. "Used in voudoun."

"Is that like, the same as a voodoo doll?" he asked.

"Voudoun is a religion," she said. "Imported from Africa and the slave trade through the Caribbean. Come over here, let me show you." She led him over to a large book on her desk called "Magic & Witchcraft: A History." She flipped it open to a section about voudoun.

Here, she said and read aloud. "A veve is a religious symbol commonly used in different branches of Voudun throughout the African diaspora, such as Haitian Voudoun." She pointed to several examples.

"There!" he said, pointing to one of them.

The caption said "Veve of Baron Samedi." It was a virtually identical depiction of the image on the scrap of paper in his bag, except that it was a photograph of a colorful version painted on the ground.

Underneath it, the caption said "In ritual and other formalities, a veve is usually drawn on the floor by strewing a powder-like substance, commonly cornmeal, wheat flour, bark, red brick powder, or gunpowder, though the material depends entirely upon the ritual. In Haitian Voudoun, a mixture of cornmeal and wood ash is used."

"So, what is the Baron Samedi?" he asked.

The Director said, "I'm not familiar with that one. Let's see," flipping a few pages further into the book's index. "Here it is, she said, page 129, Baron Samedi is is one of the lwa of Haitian Vodou. Samedi is a lwa of the dead."

"May I see that? "he asked.

"Certainly," she said, handing him the book for him to read further himself.

"I'm confused," he said. "Why would a scrap of paper depicting this...voodoo guy be in my garden?"

"It sounds like someone planted it there," said the Director.

"Planted it? What do you mean?"

"Well, if it was that deep, it didn't get there by accident, did it?" she asked.

"The box looked like it was down there for a long time."

"Have you found any other symbols or objects like that?" she asked him, pointing at it from a safe distance.

"I had a vision, not really a vision but I saw something on the guest bedroom wall. Let me try to draw it for you." He picked up the pamphlet of the museum and scrawled on it a circle with some letters around it and a figure inside. "This is not accurate, but it's what I can remember."

"That looks like a sigil," said the Director. "Similar to a veve, but it's like a seal for a demon. I don't recognize the one you drew but it would probably be in a grimoire."

"A what?" he asked.

"A grimoire. It's like a recipe book for witchcraft. It lists symbols used to conjure specific demons by name. It's like a veve. It's like a spirit's individual calling card, or autograph, whatever you want to call it. Their telephone number."

"Weird," he said. "So, someone would need to know these specific veves or sigils. They aren't commonly known, right? I mean, I never saw anything like that. It almost looks like a diagram for a semiconductor."

"Yeah, you'd have to know the occult or own a copy of an old grimoire. They aren't that hard to find, she said. "Not necessarily at your local Barnes & Noble, but you can definitely order them on Amazon or off eBay. We don't have any left in our gift shop. There's a whole subculture surrounding them. Kids even wear these things on sweatshirts these days. Here in Salem, you can find them all over."

"Ok, well thank you very much," he said, putting a $20 bill in the donations jar for the volunteers.

"Mr. Lawson?"

"Yes?" he replied.

"You might want to show that to the police…in case it has something to do with the body in your basement."

He looked down at the baggie. "Yes, you may be right," he said. He walked home.

"Oh, hi Marlena, I didn't see you there." George stood on his front steps with his back to the street, trying to hang an American flag from the pole mounted above their front door. When he turned around, she was standing at his front gate, chewing gum.

"Very patriotic," she said, pretending to salute. She was wearing a tight pink tank top that exposed her midriff as well as tight black yoga shorts.

"Yeah, thanks," he chuckled. "So what's new with you?"

"Me? Nothing. Just killing myself at the brewery. We are having a nice little Brewfest going tomorrow night, 2 for 1 drinks. I'd invite you, but you'd just blow me off again, wouldn't you?"

"I never blow anyone off," he said. "But it's probably not a great idea for me to hang around a brewery. You know how it is."

"Not really, but I'll take your word for it. Can't you just come by and have a soda or something? Maybe that Tim's Tonic, blech," she said, sticking out her pierced tongue.

"Oh, it's not that bad," he said. "It grows on ya, doesn't it?"

"Uh, no, it's awful," she said. "I refuse to carry it in our bar. So, where's the missus?" she asked, peering over his shoulder into their front door.

"Work," he said. "She works at the gym."

"Oh, maybe I have seen her there. What's her name?"

"Uh, Giselle."

"Great, I will look for her. I go to the gym a couple of times a week, so I will make sure I hunt her down."

"Great," he said flatly.

"What's the matter, afraid we'll want to share you?"

He gulped.

"Oh, I'm just teasing you! I will be very respectful if I see her, I promise. Cross my heart." She put her hand over her firm left breast.

"I'm sure, Marlena. Now, get out of here. You'll scare the horses."

She winked and strolled away toward the bar.

Now, George had one more thing to worry about. Marlena's flirtatiousness seemed harmless enough, but Giselle wouldn't perceive it that way. He now wished he had lied to Marlena about where Giselle worked.

POLICE

It had been two months since the grisly discovery in the basement. The news had largely died down, although they occasionally received unsolicited phone calls and e-mails, accusing them of beheading witches.

George and Giselle sat in a small private room at the police station on Margin Street. George looked around and pointed at the Salem Police Department plaque on the wall which said: "The Witch City, 1626" and showed a silhouette of a witch riding a broom. He looked up at it and smiled.

"Mint?" Tony the detective offered them as he walked in the room, holding a file folder, and closing the glass door behind him.

"No, thank you," they replied simultaneously.

"So, we finally got the results back from the lab," he said, popping a mint into his mouth and sitting down at the table across from the couple. "They had to send it to the national lab, they had never seen anything quite like it."

"And?" asked George.

"No matches. No dental, no matchable DNA, which is not surprising, given the age of the bones."

"And what is the age?" asked Giselle.

"Over two hundred and fifty years," said the detective, dramatically laying down crime scene photos and the report from the coroner.

"...Two fifty?" asked George, stunned, picking up the report.

"Yeah, give or take a half century. It seems the further they go back, the harder it is to pinpoint an exact date. But the coroner was pretty sure that the remaining teeth, the marrow rings, and the other science stuff suggests it was a woman in her fifties, probably Caribbean American or African American. Most likely a servant. She wasn't very tall or well-fed, apparently. Had a few skull fractures, but we don't think it was foul play. Hard to say, though. There were a few bones missing. No mandible, no tibia. But we can rule out missing persons. Unless we consider someone missing in the early 1700s."

"Tituba…" George whispered under his breath, trailing off.

"I'm sorry George, what did you say?" asked Tony.

"I said Tituba, "I think I have an idea who the bones might belong to."

"Do explain," said the detective, sitting forward to listen intently.

"Well," said George, taking out the plastic baggie he had at the museum and laying it on the table. "I found this stuff buried deep in our garden and it led me to do some more research at the Salem Witch Museum and up in Cambridge."

"What is it?" Tony said, picking up the baggie and examining it.

"An old pewter box. Inside were two bones, a small cross and a scrap of paper."

"You should have mentioned that at the house," said the detective. "We could have had those bones tested with the others. Never mind," he said. "We'll test them now."

"Sure," said George, handing him the baggie and box. "Also, the director of the Salem Witchcraft museum said that this paper has a veve on it. It's like a symbol that connects to a specific demon. In this case, a voodoo spirit. When I read more about our house, the property was probably somehow connected to the witch trials. There had been a slave named Tituba, who accused the others."

"Oh, right, the Crucible," said Tony. "That play is put on almost every year at the high school here."

"Right," said George. "They just put it on. There's also a movie. Tituba was a slave who confessed to witchcraft but recanted. My guess is that it was voodoo she had learned in Barbados, where she was from. This box and veve was probably hers since she kept the garden at our house back then. By the way, after the witch trials ended," George said,

"Tituba's fate was unknown. She literally disappeared from the history books. But what if she somehow ended up dead in the Ropes' cellar?"

"Another thing," said the Detective. "The skull was thirteen feet away from the rest of the remains. I measured it myself. Now, a human head weighs about eleven pounds, fully loaded. After decomposition, a skull would weigh about three. So, the only animals in a basement that could move a three-pound skull would be a large rat. So, you guys might have rats."

"Great," said Giselle.

"We'll call in the best exterminators," George said, putting his hand on her arm.

"As I said before, there were a few fractures in the skull. We can't tell if they occurred pre or post-mortem. So, again, we must assume rats gnawed at it over the years. There were a few old books that were found in the room near her head. Very old. Like medieval old. I can't tell if they are handwritten or were printed. They aren't in English, so maybe you'll want to get them translated. Here they are," he said, going to a cabinet and unlocking it and handing four books encased in evidence bags to George.

"These were in that room too?"

"Yeah, located next to the skull. So, while we can assume rats moved the skull, would they have also dragged all four books all the way across the room? Maybe. Now, if I recall, you said that the cement that was used to wall that up in the basement was more recent?"

"Yeah," said George. "It's a type of cement called Rosendale. It's pretty rare and was used mostly in the late 1800's. I don't think it was used before then. The Brooklyn Bridge is made of it. The base of the Statue of Liberty, that kind of stuff."

"So, that doesn't fit because then someone walled it up centuries after Tituba died? Doesn't make sense."

"It doesn't," said George. "Plus, the building was built in 1720. Tituba went missing in 1694."

"We'll definitely have to let the historians and the witch museum know about all this," the detective said, closing the file folder. "Going to make a hell of a book," Tony smirked. "But I think we can consider any criminal case closed, since there's no strong evidence of foul play plus given the age of the skeleton, and assuming a rat moved the skull as well as the books. While that's a weird set of assumptions, I don't know that we have anything else to justify an ongoing criminal investigation. Technically, there's no statute of limitations on murder in the Commonwealth, but I don't think we can even consider this a cold case. At least not right now."

"Oh yeah, I almost forgot." the detective continued. "We took some photos of the chalk writing on the floor. Have no idea what it means, but maybe you'll want to work this up when you talk to the scholars about your Tituba theory.

"Thanks, I will," said George.

"So what now?" asked Giselle. "What happens to her?" She pointed at the photo of the skull and bones.

"We removed all the fragments and dirt underneath her and sent it all over to Harvard," said the detective. "After further testing, I think they plan on interring her down at the Old Burying Ground with a ritual or service or something. You can feel free to use your basement again. We left the chalk markings on the floor since there was no point to disturbing them. They've been photographed, so you can just sweep them up, if you want.

"And the last thing, which I hate to bring up, but…"

"What is it?" asked George.

"We still can't figure out how someone set a fire in a room that was sealed. There was no oxygen to sustain kindling. When the lab analyzed the ash, they said it was freshly burnt incense and wood shavings. Modern wood. So, somehow, this new material got into the middle of a sealed room and set itself on fire. And we also still can't figure out how you were able to smell smoke from the basement in the bedroom on the second floor. Got any theories?"

George silently thought about it for a minute. "No, I really don't," he said.

"Anything else you want to tell us?" Tony asked, shooting a glance at Giselle and back at George.

"What do you mean?" asked George.

"Your wife told us that you may have bumped your head recently. Breathed in some fumes, maybe?"

"Oh, that?" George laughed, looking over at Giselle uncomfortably. "That was nothing. I thought I had opened the window, but I must have forgot. It was nothing."

"Ok, if we find out anything else, we'll let you know, and you please do the same, ok?" He handed Giselle his card.

"Yes, of course," said Giselle, picking it up and putting away snugly in her purse.

"Thank you for coming down," the detective said, standing up and opening the door for them.

"No problem, thank you, Detective," said Giselle, smiling and walking out.

"Oh and George?" said Tony.

"Yes?"

"Fix your alarm. You don't need to have it call all three branches of the armed forces if a baseball breaks your window," he winked. "Save DEFCON 1 for a real emergency, ok?"

"Ok," George laughed, embarrassed.

DINNER

"I'll have the filet rare, with *au poivre,* and a side of creamed spinach, thank you," George ordered at Rockafellas, an upbeat restaurant and bar on Essex Street walking distance from their house.

"An aristocrat," Giselle joked. The waitress smiled.

"Yes, and I will have the large seafood salad, thank you," said Giselle.

"Anything to drink?" asked the young waitress.

"I will have a pinot grigio," said Giselle. "George, are you ok with that?"

"Yeah, sure," he said, nodding emphatically. "No problem. I'm ok," he told the waitress. "I have my own water bottle," he said, pointing at it. She went off and brought Giselle's wine.

They sat at an outside table overlooking the sidewalk on a warm Friday evening on their first dinner date in years. Melissa was staying at her friend's house for the night.

"Hon, I really just want to thank you," he said.

"For what?" asked Giselle, sipping her white wine.

"For putting up with me, for the house, for...everything."

"Yeah, well, it's been a tough year so far, George, I won't tell you it hasn't."

He took her hand in his. "I really thought life was going to get easier when we sold Matthews Circle. It didn't."

"We were happy. I just want to be on record saying that. We didn't need to move here, you did. But here we are, so let's move on," she said, pulling her hand back.

"What do you think about the house? And Salem? Honestly," asked George, hesitatingly.

She chortled. "Yeah, great house, George. First, you think it's cursed or haunted or whatever. You're hearing spooky sounds and seeing things. Our window gets broken. You're digging up voodoo dolls in the garden from a dead slave whose rotting corpse was probably in our basement. But at least the water pressure is good," she said smiling.

"Yeah, maybe I should have done a little more due diligence before buying it, huh?" he laughed nervously.

Giselle laughed. "I hear that Dahmer's house is on the market. Lovely little place with a patio and renovated kitchen," she said.

He laughed loudly. "Now that's the girl I married," he said. "That's the thing about these old towns, though. They do have character."

Giselle laughed again. "That's certainly one way to put it."

The couple sat in silence for a while.

"Mel is starting to settle in, don't you think?" he asked.

"Yeah," said Giselle, looking away and sipping her wine. "I think so. We were hitting our stride before the basement incident, but kids are resilient. I told her to make a joke about it at school. Break the ice, you know?"

"Yeah," he laughed. "I heard a rumor that several of the mothers in the PTA are practicing witches. Probably in the same coven, so it's not like a body in your basement disqualifies us socially. Hell, might even play to our advantage," he chuckled. "Maybe we can sell tickets."

"Yeah," she said. "This is definitely an interesting place," he said, staring at a woman walking by while wearing a full witch costume. This place really takes it to a new level, doesn't it? Witch capital of the world, isn't that what the police badge says?"

"Yeah, it's pretty remarkable," he said. "This place took a tragedy that happened three centuries ago and embraced it. Most places would have wanted to forget about something like that Now, it's part of American history, you know? The term witch hunt has really become part of the language, even. Just ask the President," he said.

She chuckled. "Yeah, it's true. Well, let me ask you something."

"Sure," he said, intrigued.

"Are *you* happy? I mean, we moved halfway across the country to some godforsaken town, are you really happy now?"

"Yeah, I mean, I didn't expect, you know, to find a dead body in the cellar, but I feel energized here. Can't really explain it. Sometimes I wonder if I didn't live here in a past life, or someplace like it. You ever have that feeling?"

"Like déjà vu?" she asked.

"Yeah. When we were back in Chicago, I never told you this, I had a dream of this place. The house looked a little different, it was closer to the street and the water and seemed even bigger, but it was the same place. When I came here and wandered in during the open house, I had to buy it. It was like I was reconnecting with something. I never told you that."

"Not sure that is helping your case, George," she chuckled. "Buying a house that you had a vague dream about in a place you had never visited before."

"Yeah," he chuckled. "True enough."

"Who did you hear it from?" she asked.

"What?"

"You said you heard a rumor that a few of the moms were witches. Who did you hear that from?"

"Oh, Marlena," he said. "And Tim."

"Who?" she asked.

"Marlena owns the microbrewery next door and Tims owns the soda shack."

She stopped and looked at him. "Yeah, you mentioned Tim and that horrible soda. But Marlena? Brewery?"

"Oh, stop!" he said emphatically. "I told you that I met Tim on Halloween handing out sodas. He introduced me to Marlena, she is our neighbor," he said. "She's probably a witch herself," he said. "And I never once set foot in that place. So, stop," he said.

"Ok, I just would have thought you'd have mentioned her in passing."

"Nothing worth mentioning. In fact, I will introduce you to Tim later, if you want."

"And Marlena?"

"Sure, if you want, although I'm not sure you'd like her much," he said.

"Why is that?"

"She is quirky and owns a bar, basically. Not really someone you'd like, I suspect." He had no intention of introducing the two women. Nothing good could come from that interaction, he suspected.

The waitress brought their food over and placed the plates in front of them.

"So, there's one more thing I wanted to talk to you about," George said, cutting his steak and taking a bite.

"What's that?" asked Giselle.

"I'm digging up the rest of the garden to look for more clues," he said while chewing.

She put her salad fork down on the table with a clang.

"Check please," she said, signaling abruptly to the waitress.

99

GRIMOIRES

After their dinner date went south, George slept on the couch. He had hoped the couple might have another romantic evening with Melissa sleeping over at her friend's house. That was now impossible, given Giselle's reaction to his latest announcement.

"I guess it's just you and me again tonight, old boy," he said, as he patted Bailey's head and rubbed behind his ears. The dog looked up at him sympathetically.

He pulled out the professor's book and decided to skim it for any further references to Tituba, but he couldn't find any. He sat up, rubbed his eyes, and grabbed his iPad. He downloaded Arthur Miller's play the Crucible to his Kindle app, and started skimming it, as well.

There were several references to Tituba's practice of voodoo which may have followed her from Barbados. Miller himself noted in his comments that no historians definitively knew what happened to Tituba after the trials.

He kept thinking about their basement and decided to get the books that had been found down there with the body. He unsealed the evidence bag and picked out the first one which was called *Malleus Maleficarum*.

On the inside of the book was the name "J. Hale" handwritten in faded ink. The book was very old, and it had a series of Roman numerals on the frontispiece.

George didn't know how to calculate them in his head, so he typed then into the Google search bar.

1487? That can't be, he thought to himself. *This house was built in*

1720. Why would there be books that were already 230 years ago walled up in the basement?

He put the words Malleus Maleficarum into Google. The first hit was a listing on Wikipedia.

> The Malleus Maleficarum, usually translated as the Hammer of Witches, is the best-known treatise on witchcraft. It was written by the Catholic clergyman Heinrich Kramer (under his Latinized name Henricus Institoris) and first published in the German city of Speyer in 1486. It endorses extermination of witches and for this purpose develops a detailed legal and theological theory. It has been described as the compendium of literature in demonology of the 15th century. The top theologians of the Inquisition at the Faculty of Cologne condemned the book as recommending unethical and illegal procedures, as well as being inconsistent with Catholic doctrines of demonology. Because the book was ultimately condemned by the Catholic Church, some critics have noted that it contains a startling amount of information about witchcraft and the occult.

> The Witches' Hammer contains a shocking amount of detailed information for its readers to learn about the details of how to *perform* witchcraft. It has always seemed odd that the handbook ostensibly designed to stamp out the occult could become the cookbook for effectively practicing it.

> By way of just a few examples, the Witches' Hammer offers details of how to perform spells, make potions and concoctions, curse enemies, and conjure specific demons by name. If one were truly committed to stamping this conduct out as blasphemous heresy, why dignify

and communicate details to hundreds of thousands of people?

And it is indeed true that many apocryphal occult books originated in the Renaissance by unknown authors within the Church itself. These books demonstrate more than a passing familiarity with doctrine and methods and may have been written by wayward priests and monks, who were the ones in society most literate in Hebrew, Greek and Latin as well as Church rituals.

He looked back at the Crucible. There was a character named John Hale who was a Reverend from the nearby town of Beverly, he vaguely recalled. He pulled out his iPad with the Crucible on it and skimmed what he could find about Hale.

He then put the iPad down and picked up a second book called the *Ars Notoria*. It also had the name Hale, but without the letter J. He typed the Latin name of this book into Google. The top listing was an English translation of the book for sale on Amazon. The explanation said that it was one of the lengthier grimoires of the medieval period, the *Ars Notoria*, commonly referred to as the Notary Art of Solomon, promised the reader a series of orations, prayers, and invocations, which could be used to secure the favor of the Christian God, enhancing the memory, eloquence, and general academic capability of the one performing such rituals.

The entry explained that it was originally its own text, based on even older sources not yet fully documented, it was wrapped up into the Lesser Keys of Solomon along with such works as the *Ars Goetia* but some editions of the latter omit this work. Prayers contained herein invoke not just the God of Christianity, but Jesus Christ and various angelic powers as well.

He grabbed the other book that was found next to the body. It was much larger and was titled *Clavicula Solomonis*. It also had the word

Hale written in the frontispiece. He typed the Latin words into Google Translate. It said, "The Key of Solomon."

While it was in Latin, there were a series of symbols that the Director of the Museum had called sigils or seals. He immediately perked up. *Maybe I didn't imagine the symbol I saw on the wall in the room upstairs!*

He quickly flipped through the book, looking at dozens and dozens of sigils. He didn't recognize any of them, but they bore a resemblance to the one he saw on the wall. They were circular, had letters surrounding them and strange figures inside.

He came across a sigil that looked almost exactly like what he remembered seeing on the wall. He was stunned, but the pieces of the puzzle started to come together.

Assuming the skeleton in the basement was Tituba, she was indeed a practicing witch, probably having learned voodoo practices in Barbados. The teenage girls in Salem may have seen or heard her practicing spells and word got around town. Maybe Tituba in fact teach the girls some of the basics of her craft. In any event, the hysteria that followed was an overreaction to exposure to the exotic religion of the enslaved woman.

But the oddity of *these* books was that they were written in Latin and looked medieval or Renaissance. Certainly, Tituba's voodoo rituals would not have required access to them, and she probably couldn't read or write English, much less Latin. No, these books looked more religious in nature, and the Amazon description seemed to suggest some connections to Christianity or even traditional Catholicism. He wondered if John Hale had some connection to these books. *Perhaps they belonged to him at some point?*

He quietly crept back down in the basement. He hadn't been down here since the police had removed the skeletal remains weeks earlier. The wall had been almost completely removed; the support structures he had put in place had done the trick.

He flipped on a large halogen floodlight the fire department had apparently left behind. He could clearly see the room now. He took out his iPhone and took several photos of the chalk markings that remained on the dirt floor. Most of it had been trampled by the many people who had visited the room to photograph and remove the remains, but several sections near the corners were undisturbed.

The lettering around the circle looked Hebrew. He snapped as many photographs as he could. He then turned off the halogen lighting and went back upstairs. He felt a chill go through his body as he climbed the stairs and closed the basement door behind him.

That night, he woke up again at 3:30 a.m., after having another nightmare. He was a boy and was trapped in a funeral home out in the desert. It was many miles away from any town. There was a wake for Giselle and Melissa and their lifeless bodies were inside of two coffins in the center of the room.

His extended family had apparently left him behind and he was forced to spend the night in the funeral parlor, as he had no phone and there was no way to communicate with anyone until they arrived back in the morning. He tried to rest, but he couldn't take his eyes off their caskets.

Suddenly, he heard a rustling sound coming from inside one of them. He laid there, terrified that one of the coffins would burst open. Just then, he heard a knock from inside the coffin, even though he was totally alone in the building.

When he awoke, he was drenched in sweat and his heart was palpitating. It took him over and hour and a half to get back to sleep.

PLANS

"You're doing what, now?" asked Giselle, sounding exasperated while the couple stood in their backyard.

"Building a workspace, I had told you I was going to do that when we moved in, remember?"

"Uh yeah, but now you want to put your stuff where a dead woman was found? You don't think that's just a little creepy?" she said, as she sprayed her flowers with a garden hose.

"I figured it was out of the way, and I won't bother anyone with noise or whatever."

"Are you ok, George? Seriously. First, you started the room renovation upstairs, that ended well. My mother never came for Easter, after we found a body in the basement. You dug up half the yard, and now you want to destroy the rest." She pointed at the half-destroyed garden.

"I really am starting to wonder about you. Maybe you should see a doctor, get that MRI?"

"Oh, for Christ's sake, why is everything always about my flaws?" he asked angrily. "You accuse me of drinking again, you seemed to say I was cheating with the bar owner next door, what's next? Am I embezzling funds at work?"

"Oh, stop being so melodramatic," she said dismissively. "Go ahead and build your little man cave, but you know, don't drag us into your wacko issues."

"Issues? I have issues because I want a space in my own basement. I mean, I paid for this house, I think I can have some say in it!"

"Speaking of funds," Giselle said, turning off the garden hose temporarily. "How did you pay for this house? I realized that you funded it before we settled on the house in Chicago. How did you pay for it?"

"I drew down on my 401(k), but I put the money back," he said quietly.

"You did what?" she asked angrily.

"Yeah, I took out most of it, but I put most of it back."

"Wait, wait," she said, putting up her hand. "You took all the money…"

"Not all—" he interrupted.

"Ok, most of the money—that was in *my* retirement account, and bought a house without me seeing it?"

"Well, it's technically our retirement accounts," he muttered.

"What did you say?" she demanded furiously.

"Nothing, but I will make back the ten percent tax penalty on withdrawal in a couple of years at most. The real estate market here is hot, and ten percent appreciation won't take long."

She silently went back to watering the garden, contemplating the latest revelations. George skulked back into the house and decided now might be a good time to take a long walk.

"You'll want this one," the young woman with pink hair and a pentagram tattoo on her arm said, handing George a book titled Mastering Witchcraft. The woman who stood at the counter at the Crow Haven Bookstore looked every inch a budding Millennial witch. "Oh, and this one, too." She handed him another book.

"And how would I talk to someone who has been dead for like, let's say, three hundred years?" George asked her, whispering.

"With the right supplies," the girl said, as though she was a pharmacist dispensing routine aspirin.

"Necromantic incense," she said, as she reached for a pre-filled sachet to place on top of the book. "A few black candles, some salt. Here…" She reached for a pre-packaged kit called "Raising Hell."

"I see you're prepared for these requests," George joked.

"People mostly want three spells," she said. "The most popular is a love spell," she said pointing to a whole display of red candles and heart-shaped trinkets.

"Not surprised," said George, eyeing the display counter full of kits.

"Revenge or protection, number two, and speaking with the dead is third. But usually, it's a dead grandfather or mother, not a 300-year-old shade. That is tougher."

"Why is that?" he asked, amused.

"The dead can speak to the living until they dissipate. Once their energy's recycled, they've moved on. Unless they were a particularly powerful spirit who can last centuries to you and me. Of course, time is different to the dead."

"Right," said George. "Makes sense, I guess."

"But you need to know something?"

"What's that?" he asked.

"Summoning shades is dangerous. Worse than conjuring demons."

"Why is that?" he asked.

"We're meant to move on. If you drag the dead back into our world, they can get reattached. Then you can't get rid of them. They need to draw life energy, like a vampire. Even experienced witches won't do it."

"Right, ok. Thanks for the heads-up," he said flippantly. "By the way, how do you know all this stuff?"

"YouTube and oh, my mother is a witch," she said, pointing at a black-haired woman at the cash register.

He chuckled. "How much do I owe you?" he smiled.

"Your soul," she replied.

"Come again?"

"$53.95. Just a joke."

"Right," George said, taking out his wallet. "In other words, here's my credit card," he smirked.

After visiting the occult bookstore, George drove over to Home Depot and checked his iPhone. He had made a list of the items that he would need to construct a workspace in the basement. He bought a small pile of lumber and other materials and lugged them back home in his trunk. He thought it might be best to avoid Giselle for a little longer.

He went downstairs without saying anything to her and started to assemble a crude desk in the main part of the basement. He then placed it in the empty room where Tituba's body had been found. What he hadn't wanted to reveal to Giselle was that he felt a connection to this room despite the fact it was essentially a one-person cemetery for a long time.

He shifted his makeshift workbench toward the wall, although he knew the reaction it would engender from Giselle if she saw it. He also installed a thick wooden door that would seal the room completely shut and allow him to lock it from both inside and outside, to maintain complete privacy. His only concern was that he calculated that there would only be about an hour of oxygen (at most) for him to breathe while inside the room with the door shut. He made a note to keep a timer going on his iPhone or iPad.

He put together a bookcase that would display the old grimoires that had previously been found there by the police. He had also purchased over a dozen modern books about the witch trials and the occult on Amazon and eBay, at the witch museum bookshop and a few other used bookstores in Salem and Boston. He was particularly excited about a new translation of the Witches' Hammer he was able to locate, as well as translations of the Latin grimoires into English.

He perched his iPad on the workspace which would allow him to monitor all the exterior and interior video cameras and motion sensors in the house simultaneously, as well as do any additional Internet research.

Finally, he ran a heavy-duty extension cord from the cellar's main electrical outlet to a plug strip that would allow him to keep a tiny refrigerator to keep his seltzer cold and to plug desk lamps into. He drilled a hole in the rafter beam to run the wire through. He made sure not to place anything in the nine-foot circular space that had been previously chalked out on the dirt floor.

He admitted to himself that the result was a macabre arrangement of makeshift furniture in a concrete room with no windows in the back of their basement. But for his purposes it was perfect.

His theory was that Tituba's spirit was connected to this space, with her bones having lain here for centuries. He was going to experiment with summoning her, to learn if she had placed a hex on this house—and why. In doing so, he might try to figure out how to remove it.

Deep down, he knew that this scheme was bizarre. He had spent the better part of his adult life as an educated engineer studying complex devices, plans and blueprints. He hadn't thought about anything paranormal—or even religious—since he was a kid. But after speaking with Mike, they just couldn't figure out why this property could have possibly accounted for dozens and dozens of strange and untimely deaths. Now that he found concrete evidence of a linkage between Tituba, voodoo, and black magic on these grounds, he was convinced this was the way to go.

And who was to say that black magic wasn't real? As the books had elegantly explained, modern science provided merely a dim circle of light around a campfire. When one wandered outside the seeming safety of the firelight, dark shadows beyond invoked a primordial terror that could not be so easily escaped. He was convinced that an unorthodox approach would reveal the secrets of this house's mysterious past. And if it didn't, so what? What was the harm?

Sure, the old books had warned that necromancy—the dark of summoning the shades of the dead—is among the most dangerous occult practices. George wasn't sure why, though. As an altar boy, he always found it interesting that Catholics fervently prayed to saints, who really weren't anything more than dead Catholics who were spiritually and highly moral people while alive.

He supposed that the only difference was that he would be praying or speaking to a former slave who had been dead for centuries and who may have had the power, while alive, to place an intergenerational hex on this property. Such a woman might have been a force to reckon with alive. Now dead for centuries, if her angry soul was still around, she might be ornery. And how would he even communicate with a ghost? How would he know she might be listening? He had no idea what he was doing.

And he still couldn't believe it had gotten to this point. A year ago, he was sitting on a pool deck outside Chicago, drinking seltzer and listening to the wind blow through the backyard pines. Now, here he was, in the basement of an old, cursed mansion in Salem, conjuring shades of the dead. It was so absurd and bizarre, it almost felt like it had all been a strange dream.

He had looked it up in the index and the books suggested that he perform the rituals on a new moon. Since that was still a week away, he would get all the preparations in order, and keep this room locked.

SHADE

After Giselle had fallen asleep, on the night of the new moon, George snuck out of the bedroom and silently closed the bedroom door behind him. He crept down two flights of stairs to the cellar.

He unlocked the padlock on the outside of the door to his secret workspace. He closed it behind him and locked it from the inside so no one could accidentally walk in on him. Not that anyone would even know he was in there—even with a light on inside the room and the rest of the cellar pitch black.

If Giselle awakened and looked for him, she would assume he was elsewhere. Even if she even explored the basement, which was extremely unlikely, the door was locked from the inside. He set his iPhone alarm setting for 45 minutes, as he suspected that there might not be more than an hour of oxygen in the room at most. If he needed to, he could unlock the door to let some fresh air in, and then lock it again.

He had already prepared for the ritual. He re-traced the symbols on the floor with white chalk that he had bought at a local toy store. Typically, this chalk was used by children to write on a sidewalk, but it seemed to work effectively on the hard dirt floor.

He had no idea what the weird symbols meant. From what he read, the drawing of a circle on the floor created a wall of protection against an attack. He didn't know what could possibly attack him or how a circle in chalk might possibly work to negate that. But as an engineer, he believed in following directions carefully.

He placed the black candles in the four corners of the cardinal directions. He assembled various implements on the small table in the center of the circle. They were supposed to be his ritual tools. He had finally figured out what the religious objects in the cellar might have been used for. One was an incense burner; another was a cup to hold the incense.

He removed all his clothes and placed them on a chair. This was one of the stranger aspects of the ritual. The books had called this being 'skyclad' – a fancy way of saying nude. But since the room was isolated, he didn't feel too awkward, and he kept his pile of clothes nearby in case he needed to get dressed in a hurry.

He opened the book he had purchased and began to read the ritual of necromancy. First, he faced the eastern side of the house facing the door and read aloud: "All wise eagle, great ruler of tempests, storms and whirlwinds and master of the heavenly vault. Great prince of the powers of the air. Be present, I pray of thee and guard my circle from all perils approaching from the east."

He turned toward the south wall and read: "O Lion, Lord of lightning, master of the sun, great prince and power of fire. Be present, I pray of thee, and guard this circle from all perils approaching from the south."

He turned toward the west and said aloud: "Serpent of old. Ruler of the deep. Guardian of the bitter sea. Prince of the power of water. Be present, I pray of thee and guard this circle from all perils approaching from the west."

He then turned toward the north wall of the cellar: "Black bull of the north. Dark ruler of mountains and of the dirt that lies beneath them. Prince of the powers of earth, be present I pray of thee and guard this circle from all perils approaching from the north.

He returned to the center of the circle, looked down at the book and read: "I, George Henry Lawson, hereby surround myself within this circle of protection, around which are written the sacred names of God. Across this boundary, no hostile power dare set its foot. So mote it be!"

He felt a strange sensation uttering these words. He had never said anything quite like it before. The last time he had said anything like this was back when he was an altar boy praying the Our Father at Mass. But this was a completely different feeling. He really had no idea what he was saying, but the words felt powerful, strong, and weighty. It gave him a tingle from saying something so odd and profound aloud.

The book said that his circle of protection was now empowered, 'charged,' it had said. He then turned to the pages involving the rite of necromancy. On the center of the table, he placed a piece of paper on which he had written the name "TITUBA" across it.

At the bookstore, he had purchased the kit of incense that contained wormwood, church incense, dittany of Crete into which he had dripped a few drops of honey and olive oil. Finally, he took a small Swiss Army knife and cut his finger so that a few drops of his own blood dripped into it. He ignited the charcoal tablet using a lighter and sucked on his finger.

The instant that the charcoal lit, he smelled the incense burning and it struck him all at once. This was precisely the smell that had triggered the smoke alarm and summoned the police and fire department previously.

He took a seat in the chair and looked down at his iPhone. He had approximately 40 minutes left before the oxygen might run out in this room. He could always open the door to get some fresh air, but he suddenly realized something: the smoke of the incense might set off the smoke detector. That would wake up the whole house, and indeed, the whole block (again). He had forgotten to de-activate it. In any event, there was no going back now.

He held the light from the iPhone over the book and read aloud the strange words it contained.

Colpriziana Offina Alta Nestera Fuaro Menut
I name thee Tituba. Thou Art Tituba.

He wasn't sure what to do next. The book said nothing except to provide additional instructions in the event nothing happened. He waited ten minutes, and looked around the room. The candles barely flickered, as the only movement of air in the room was from his breathing.

After that, he concluded that nothing had happened and continued reading aloud.

> *Spirit of Tituba, thou mayest now approach the gates of the east to answer truly my liege demands. Berald Baroald, Balbini, Gab Gabor Agaba! Arise, Arise, I charge and command thee.*

He waited another ten minutes. Again, nothing seemed to happen. He wasn't even sure what was supposed to happen, but the book said that if the room was still, the person should finally read the following in a loud and authoritative voice, tapping the picture with his finger after each phrase.

> *By the mysteries of the deep, tap, by the flames of Banal, tap, by the powers of the east, tap, and by the silence of the night. By the holy rites of Hecate, tap, I conjure and exorcise thee, tap, Tituba, to present thyself here and answer truly my demands, tap. So mote it be!*

Now he waited. He really had gone quite a long distance through this ritual process, without knowing what he expected to happen anyway. Maybe, he figured, it would be dramatic like the movies. Maybe Tituba would just suddenly show up wearing chains like Jacob Marley, and tell him all about Christmases past, present and future in the Ropes Mansion. It seemed absurd, but then again, so was summoning the shade of a dead slave by using black magic that he read about in a book he purchased for $22.95 up the street.

A few minutes after he finished saying the final words from the book, his iPhone screen went black, and the flashlight application turned off. His battery had run out, which was hard to fathom given that it was fully charged only a half hour ago. True, he had the flashlight function on the whole time, but that alone shouldn't have eaten up the entire battery charge that quickly.

He desperately pressed the power button and held it down hard. The phone battery was completely dead, and he had forgotten to bring a charger. He had no idea how much oxygen was left in the room because it was the only timer. The light remaining in the room was from the four candles and the smoldering incense which was emitting a lot of smoke. The four candles gave off ample light, however.

He started to feel woozy. He realized that he had made some big errors in his calculations. There would have been approximately 45 minutes to an hour of oxygen to breathe in the sealed fifteen by fifteen-foot room, normally. But the candles and incense were consuming some of that, as well.

If he opened the door to the main part of the cellar too soon, the smoke would undoubtedly set off the smoke detector. In fact, that may happen anyway. But if he waited to do so, he might pass out. If he went unconscious, he might very well die in here, since the door was locked from the inside and no one even knew that he was down in here. They might not find his body for days. When he had fainted from the paint thinner, Giselle said he had "slept" the whole day away.

He quickly blew out three of the four candles to conserve oxygen. He was now plunged into near total darkness and realized that he would need to find the key to the padlock to open the door.

Just then, he felt an icy breeze from the east side of the room and the final candle was blown out.

That is impossible. This room is sealed and must be at least 80 degrees inside from the flames and his body heat. There is no way a cold breeze could pass through here.

He reached for the lighter he had used to light the charcoals so he could re-light a candle. But it wasn't there. He rummaged around and could feel the open books, the incense burner and his Swiss army knife on the floor and table. But no lighter.

The situation was now becoming serious. If he couldn't find the lighter, he might not find the key. He wondered if he just forget about the light and look for the key. He started crawling around on his hands and feet, figuring that the key might be near the lighter and he would be fine if he found either. But he found neither.

He was now in full blown panic. The absurdity of the situation struck him. Here he was, an educated engineer at 50 years old, crawling around in the dirt in the basement of a mansion where he was up at three o'clock in the morning, trying to summon the dead—and it wasn't going very well. But there would be plenty of time for ruminating on the absurdity once he could get the hell out of the mess he had created.

The room was getting even stuffier now. The smoke from the incense seemed to have gotten thicker and extinguishing the candles might have consumed more oxygen than if he had left them all burning. He cursed at himself for being so short sighted. For an engineer, poor planning was a mortal sin. All these factors could have been anticipated and avoided.

As he crawled around in the darkness, the only light that flickered was from the charcoal ingots. For an instant in the thick smoke wafting upward from the glowing charcoals, he could have sworn that he saw something move.

A strange gravelly sound seemed to come from the brazier. He figured it was probably the fiery hot coals reacting with the honey, olive oil or his blood. But the sound seemed to be getting louder.

For an instant, he asked himself a terrifying question: *What if these strange words succeeded in making something happen? What the hell would I do now?*

As he fumbled around, he accidentally knocked the brass brazier onto the dirt. The incense spilled and caught fire just enough to give off another flicker of light. He could have sworn in that instant that he saw a shadow move on the west wall. It seemed inkier than the darkness surrounding it.

Just beyond it, he saw something glint in the dirt by the far wall. It was the key. He lunged for it. It was now under dirt that he had accidentally kicked up. He scrambled all around, desperately feeling for it. He looked up and saw that the amorphous shadow seemed to have slid from the west wall onto the north wall.

He grabbed the key and brushed off the dirt. He ran toward the east and fumbled for the padlock and finally got the key inside of it. It unlatched. He pushed open the door and ran for the smoke detector to yank all the wires out of it before it could activate the security system.

He reached for the light switch on the wall and tripped into one of the holes that remained in the basement, and which he had forgotten to fill in. He got up, rubbing his bloody knee. Once he reached the light switch, he flipped it on.

When the glare of the LED's turned on, he felt ridiculous. Here he stood, naked, with a bruised knee, coughing in his smoky cellar, holding the wires to a broken smoke detector. He would need a shower before he could get into bed, as he was filthy, and his hair and clothes now smelled of smoke and incense.

CAB

At 6 a.m., George finally stepped outside their front door. He was exhausted. He sat on the steps, drinking seltzer, and checking his iPhone. There were over thirty unread messages from yesterday from his work colleagues. They would all have to wait.

The ritual had been a disaster. While Giselle slept, he was up until nearly 5 a.m. trying to clean up the mess in the basement. He disabled the security system and had to set up a fan to draw the smoke out of the cellar and out the back door before it could waft upward into the house.

He washed his clothes by hand in a utility sink with Palmolive so that they wouldn't smell weird in the laundry. He had to put several band aids on his finger which he had cut deeply with the Swiss Army knife. He had accomplished nothing.

As he sat on the steps, he saw a yellow cab with the company name Witch City Taxi painted on it slowly driving by. The sign on top said it was vacant, so he hailed it. The driver stopped and rolled down the window.

"Hi, where you headed this early?" he asked.

"Around town, I just need some air, ok?"

"Hop in," said the elderly man, flipping his meter to on.

George hopped in the back seat.

"Hi, I'm George," he said, extending his hand to shake the driver's hand.

"Fred. Where you headed again?"

"Let's start by just going around the block, Fred."

"Come again?" asked the confused driver.

"Just go down and circle around the block," he said.

"Ok, your dime," he said slowly now driving down Essex Street.

George opened the rear passenger side window.

"You live in the Ropes?" the driver asked.

"Yep, moved in a while ago," replied George, opening the driver's side window to breathe in the fresh morning air.

"Ah, the Madhouse."

"That's certainly what I've learned to call it," confessed George.

"You had…anything happen in there yet?"

"Other than the rotting corpse we found in the basement?" George chuckled.

"I forgot that was down there. You guys handling that ok?"

"Not really. My wife thinks I'm nuts, which I may be."

"Oh my God, you're becoming a celebrity around here. Remind me where you're from?"

"Chicago."

"Ah, ok. That might explain it," he laughed. George laughed too.

The driver circled the block as George requested, over, and then repeatedly, answering all the questions that George asked him; questions concerning the town's history, and how long he had been working as a driver, and if he had once carried any of the previous owners of the mansion, and what he knew about the Madhouse.

When George decided that the pointless trip was over, he was charged only a $1.25 fare, but he paid the driver $5, in return for his "cooperation". The man watched George walk back into the Madhouse, looking over his shoulder and his sides in paranoia, and shook his head in pity, before counting his money and driving away from the mansion.

PROJECT

George sat in a stuffy conference room on the 26th floor of an office building overlooking Boston Harbor with a team of a dozen other engineers, lawyers, and city planners. The floor to ceiling windows allowed a maximum of light in, although today was overcast.

He was thoroughly exhausted from being up all night with the bizarre, failed ritual, and he had totally forgotten about today's important meeting. He was grumpy and ill-tempered. He hadn't shaved in weeks, so his beard was scraggly and unkempt. He had forgotten to wear a suit. He drank several cups of coffee to keep him awake, but they only made him worse.

"I have no idea why the city is holding the plans up," he told the team again. "Tom, can't you tell us anything further?"

Tom Kessler, the Boston Planning & Development Agency representative sat on the far side of the table, looking every bit a disinterested civil servant. He wore a crumpled suit, twenty-year old tie, and plaid dress shirt.

"I told you already, George," he said sheepishly. "I spoke to the vendor and supplier diversity specialist, and she said that the Procurement Manager needs to coordinate with both the Project Manager and the Contract Administrator to ensure compliance with all the terms and conditions and to ensure a diverse vendor pool."

"What the hell does that mean?" asked George, frustrated by Tom's use of lingo.

"—George, please," interrupted his friend and supervisor Mark.

"Tom, we are just really concerned. We fell way behind schedule on getting the convention center renovation approved, and Mr. Friedman is considering pulling out entirely. Can't we just get an ETA on the approval process?" Mark asked.

"Guys, it's out of my hands. The problem is that your team," Tom said, looking around the room, "is just not diverse enough."

"Ahem," spoke up Raj, an engineer who had relocated to Boston from Bangladesh. "Am I chopped liver?"

"Diverse *enough*," repeated Tom. "Boston requires that a certain minimum number of minority-owned and women-owned vendors be appointed. We can't overlook important requirements because your client is in the unique position of having an internal deadline."

"So, what do we tell our client?" asked George.

Tom stood up and gathered his papers into his briefcase. "Tell them to hire a better engineering firm next time."

"Prick," said George. The room went silent.

"Have a nice day," said Tom Kessler, opening and then slamming the conference room door closed behind him.

"Jesus Christ, George, you just flipped off the City of Boston, do you realize that? Tom was supposed to be our man on the inside. The *inside*. He worked for us. Now, we are at his mercy. He can just tell the city planners to kill the deal, and Friedman will fire us. Are you happy?" He slammed his coffee mug down on the marble table.

"No, I'm not happy, but this is bullshit. Can't you see that? They are using that diversity crap to hire their buddies. It's corruption. Typical Boston. It's why you guys couldn't get the big dig done."

"Oh yeah, in Chicago, you guys were squeaky clean," said Mark, sarcastically.

"No, but we got the job done," said George. "We knew who to grease. In this city, you need to give Harvard handjobs to get a project finished."

"Yeah, well, maybe you should work elsewhere, George."

"Yeah, maybe I should," George said, stomping out of the room.

George wasn't sure if he still had a job. He had grabbed his bag from his office and left the building. He strongly suspected that Mark was hinting that he should seriously consider finding another job by making such a comment in a crowded room. If the City denied, or continued to indefinitely delay, the project, Mr. Friedman probably would cancel the plans to renovate the convention center. Friedman was a major client for the engineering firm, and the team would undoubtedly look for a scapegoat if the deal fell apart. Since George was the last guy hired, he would probably be the first to be fired and blamed.

But rightly so, he silently admitted to himself. Even with the whole diversity push, he had spent countless hours researching and investigating the history of the Ropes Mansion, rather than perfecting the submissions to the city planning committees. Back in Chicago, he was a Type A lunatic with his submissions. If there was a single typographical error, he would have stayed up all night getting it done perfectly—and gone out for drinks with the client to cement relationships.

But recently, he had stopped caring so much about his work. He also knew he had placed Mark in an impossible situation, and Mark had warned him back at the Yankees-Sox game that this would happen with the Friedman project if he screwed around too much. Yet he couldn't help it.

He hadn't slept in two days, and yet, despite possibly being unemployed for the first time in his career, his mind drifted back to the house and its history again.

PIER

It was still summer, and the weather had stayed hot, at least by Massachusetts' standards. He had personally modified his electric car to suit his own convenience, and to keep Giselle from driving it around and messing with it, like she had done a long time ago back in the Midwest. It served him well, and his drive was easy and smooth. Rather than going straight home, he decided to stop at the pier and grab a hot dog and enjoy the warm weather. He felt a million miles away from work there, and he could forget about the fact that he was now probably unemployed after the stunt he pulled at the meeting.

He continued to find it so odd that Charles had committed suicide after walking down to the pier from the Mansion. It was such a pleasant spot, he found it hard to believe that anyone could make such a fatal decision so soon after visiting it. He wanted to retrace the man's steps, to try to gain some insight into what Charles must have thought and felt visiting the pier after hearing of his son's death in the Pacific theater of World War II.

Approaching the parking lot next to the water, he suddenly spotted a figure standing next to the shore, at the edge of the pier. As he slowly inched closer, the figure's face focused to reveal Charles' face, which he had seen in the picture he found, staring at him. George was flabbergasted; so shocked, in fact, that he screamed and swerved off the path and drove his car straight off the boat ramp and into the water.

The car started to sink fast, and he with it. He struggled to unbuckle his seat belt and get out, but he had also personally modified the locks, and couldn't get them to open as the car quickly filled up with dark water that was now rushing in from all sides.

He desperately grabbed a wrench tool from under his driver's seat and managed to crack the driver's side window. It was shatterproof, so he had to strike it again and again in the same place with the metal wrench. It finally shattered into a thousand small pieces which covered him. Using his arms, he dragged his body up and shimmied out of the window. He was momentarily thankful for having worked out so much as the upper body strength may have just saved his life. But after climbing out, he lacked enough strength to swim back to the surface and he felt himself starting to sink again. His wet jeans felt like they weighed a ton.

He would have drowned, were it not for a teenage boy working at the pier who happened to see him swerve off the road and straight over the boat ramp. The boy apparently hesitated at first but gained the courage to save him when he saw George using whatever was left of his strength to climb towards the water's surface.

The boy had jumped in off the wooden planks and was able to get George safely under his arms, but the Tesla was now at the bottom about 20 feet down. The boy told George to lay still while he ran to get some help, and George started to contemplate the gravity of everything that had just happened so quickly.

His car was gone, and he would most probably never get it back. He had insurance on it but wasn't too sure that would be of any use, considering how much he had modified the car and switched it up to serve him and him only.

He was still deep in thought on the insurance implications, when he felt something biting at his feet. He withdrew from the edge of the water to find three snapping turtles, coming out of the water and gaining on his legs. He crawled backwards as they approached, and one of them latched onto his leg, biting him multiple times until he started bleeding.

He yelled and tried to kick them off but to no avail and was rescued by a man working at the pier, whom the boy that had rescued him went to get. The turtles had slipped back into the water.

The men put him under their arms and carried him off the pier and onto dry ground. As he was being carried off, his legs bleeding, he looked back at the side of the pier where he was sure he had seen the previous owner of the Ropes Mansion. But the man was no longer there.

Surprisingly, his iPhone still worked, as it was in his pocket and was apparently water-resistant. He pulled it out and clicked on favorites to reach Giselle. He got put directly into her voicemail.

"Honey, I'm ok but I have been in a serious car accident. Call me back, I'm at the pier down the street." He hung up and hoped his message wasn't going to be too terrifying for Giselle to year. But he figured the sooner he could speak to her, the better.

"Boy, mister, what the heck just happened? How did you end up in the water like that?" asked one of the teenage boys.

"I don't...know. I must have spaced out or something. I thought I saw someone in front of my car and I guess I lost control. Is my car gone?"

"Yeah, it's at the bottom. You can still see the headlights on if you look over the pier. But the salt water will destroy the engine."

"Maybe not, it's a Tesla. Sealed engine. We'll see."

"The ambulance and police are here, mister."

Just then, an ambulance and a police cruiser pulled up.

An EMT got out of the passenger side and ran up to George. He looked George over and saw the blood on his lower legs. "Don't move, ok?"

He laid him flat on a stretcher to keep him immobilized until they could assess any serious physical injuries. Another EMT cut his pants with a pair of scissors up to his knee.

"That's where the turtle bit me," George said to him, pointing at his bloody lower legs.

"Turtle?" asked the confused EMT.

"Yeah, some snapping turtles attacked my legs as I came up out of the water."

The EMT stopped and stared at him. "Sir, are you on any drugs or were you drinking alcohol?"

"Drugs? No," George laughed. "And I haven't touched a drop of booze in ten years."

"Well, you seem to have driven off a pier and maybe hallucinated."

"Hallucinated?" asked George. "What do you mean?"

"Well, there is no such thing as turtles here. That is cold salt water, we are in Massachusetts. Your leg injuries are from scraping the wooden pier."

"Can you tell us what day it is?" asked the other EMT.

"No, I forget. Maybe Monday?"

"It's Friday, sir. Fortunately, there aren't any broken bones or serious injuries, but I think we need to bring you in for observation," said the EMT.

"I'm fine, really," insisted George. Just then, his iPhone buzzed.

"George?" asked Giselle in a terrified voice.

"Yeah, I'm ok hon. Just drove my car into the ocean."

Silence.

"What?" asked Giselle.

"Yeah, I guess I blacked out for a split second and drove off the pier. Car is gone, hon."

"Uh...wait, are you ok?" asked Giselle, thoroughly confused.

"Yeah, I guess so. My legs are a little banged up, but I'm ok. They want to bring me in for observation though. Just to be safe, I guess."

"I'll be at the pier in ten minutes," she said urgently.

"No, I'll be at the hospital by then."

"Ok, ask them where they are bringing you," she said.

"Hey, where are you taking me?"

"Salem Hospital, Mass General Brigham, it's on Highland," said the EMT. "We'll be there in five."

"The local hospital on Highland," he told her.

"Ok, I'll be right there," she said. "I love you, George."

"Love you too, hon." He hung up.

"Can I have your name and identification before we transport you, sir?" asked the other EMT who was holding a clipboard.

"Yeah, George Lawson," he said, pulling out his driver's license and insurance card.

The EMTs glanced at each other. "Hey didn't we see you at your house a few months ago? Aren't you the guy with the crazy alarm and body in your basement?"

"Yep," he said, laying there. "That would be me."

"We didn't recognize you," said one EMT. "Ok, hang on, we're loading you up now, so watch your hands." They lifted him up into the back of the ambulance and slammed the doors.

Through the back windows, he could see two policemen had congregated at the end of the pier and were apparently staring down into the water at his car.

HOSPITAL

"Good news," said Doctor Teefey, the attending physician at the emergency room. "Your husband doesn't seem to have suffered any serious physical injuries, just a few scrapes. We drew his blood, and it appears perfectly normal. However, I'd like an MRI of his brain, to be safe." The doctor stood in the waiting room, talking to Gisele and Melissa who were visibly shaken.

"Thank God. But did George tell you about the blackout?" Giselle asked nervously.

"No, he didn't." The doctor now looked more concerned. "Please come over here, it's more private. Have a seat," he offered. Gisele and Melissa sat down with him in a private area.

"We moved here recently from Chicago," Giselle said. "Right after we moved in, my husband had a strange fainting episode. We chalked it up to fumes from paint thinner in a room with the windows closed. But he was unconscious in that room for hours. He had a headache, so I thought maybe he hit his head."

"When was this?"

"A few months ago," she said.

"Ok, anything else?" asked the doctor, taking notes.

"And since then, he's been acting strange. He is paranoid, he thinks he hears noises at night. He installed a security system that he stares at all the time on his iPad. He oversleeps a lot, complains about work."

"Could be stress," suggested the doctor.

"Maybe," said Giselle, "but there's more. He dug up our garden, looking for what he called 'clues.' He thinks our house is cursed by a dead slave that was practicing voodoo. Then we had something strange happen at our house," she continued. "They found a skeleton in our basement, walled up..."

"Wow, oh yeah! I read that story in the paper. That was you guys?"

"Yep," said Melissa. "After that, Dad really lost it."

"Yeah, I guess he has," agreed Giselle.

"To be sure, that was pretty traumatic from what I read," said the doctor dismissively.

"Can I ask you a question Doctor, and please be honest?" asked Giselle.

"Of course," said the doctor.

"Did you test his blood for alcohol or drugs? George had a drinking problem."

"That's the first thing we look for when there's a single car accident. Any car accident, really. But especially one where someone has driven his car off a pier. But here, there were zero signs of drugs or alcohol. Nothing. So, then we look at neurological issues, which is why I want an MRI. What about psychiatric issues? He has never been diagnosed with any disorders, right?"

"No, he hasn't," said Giselle.

"And I assume he doesn't take any medications for anxiety or depression or schizophrenia or anything?"

"Nothing, no," she responded. "He's otherwise in great health."

"Ok, so the only thing we can really do is look at the MRI. God willing, it's clean and we can write this off as a one-time incident. But if there's anything going on, we'll see it."

"Like what exactly are you looking for?" asked Giselle.

"No point in talking about it now," said the doctor. "Let's just wait and see. We should have the MRI results in a few hours, so sit tight."

"Can we see him now?" asked Giselle.

"Absolutely. He's in 28 in the back there. Just keep him calm. The MRI will take a little bit of time, and I don't want him agitated for it."

"Ok, thank you Doctor," Giselle said. They walked into the back of the ER.

"Daddy?" Melissa ran up and hugged her father tightly.

"Hi, honey," he said.

Giselle walked over and hugged and kissed him. "How are you feeling?"

"I feel fine, really. I talked to Dr. Teefey, he said I'm fine."

"We talked to him too, he just wanted to run one more test, an MRI, to rule everything out."

"Is that really necessary?" he asked.

"Yes. After the fainting incident and now this blackout, we want to be safe," said Giselle.

"The car is gone," said George sullenly.

"I figured," said Giselle.

"Can't we just buy a new one?" asked Melissa.

"Probably. The insurance company is going to ask some hard questions for sure, though."

"Ok," Giselle said. "Don't worry about that right now."

"Did you hear about the turtles?" he asked, changing the subject abruptly.

"The turtles?" asked Melissa. Giselle shook her head and asked, "What turtles?"

"Never mind," George said. "Can you just hand me my water bottle? Thanks. I think the MRI will be done today, right?"

"Yeah," said Giselle. "The doctor said they can squeeze you in soon, but you have to lay still. I think it can take like forty minutes and you can't move the whole time."

"Ugh," he said. "That's an eternity."

"We can't lose you, George, so just be quiet and get the MRI."

Melissa hugged him again.

"Ok, ok," he said begrudgingly.

RESULTS

"What did I tell you?" asked George. "Fit as a fiddle."

"I'm honestly surprised," said Giselle to the doctor.

"Great, but how do you explain everything we talked about?" she asked Doctor Teefey.

"I don't know of any medical cause, Mrs. Lawson, but it isn't anything we picked up on the tests, so I don't really know what to tell you. I guess just keep an eye on him and follow up with his regular physician for routine follow-up tests and physicals."

"Ok," she said. "Thank you."

"You'll be discharged in a few minutes, ok? Feel better." The doctor grabbed the clipboard and walked away briskly.

"So, how do you explain it all, George?" Giselle asked her husband. "You drove your car off the pier into the ocean after blacking out."

"I just lost control of it," he said. "Honestly, between you and me, I think I screwed it up when I messed with the computer settings. I think the brakes were lagging or something. Before I knew it, the car was sliding down the boat ramp. They really need to put up a barrier so that doesn't happen again. I might actually write a letter about that."

Deep down, though, George remained silently convinced that he saw the spirit of the former owner of the Mansion on the pier that day. But he could not tell anyone that. They'd have him in a strait jacket. One might expect that George's near-death experience at the pier would be enough to make him reflect on his current way of life, and try to do things differently, but it only seemed to intensify his drive.

He was now definitely sure that there was something going on behind the scenes. That experience was everything he needed to pull it all together. It made him too sure. He was convinced he wasn't crazy. He was convinced that there was someone trying to stop him from figuring the truth out, from unraveling the mystery. To him, now, it was all like a race. A game.

His working theory was that someone had built this house knowing about Tituba's curse. The Ropes Mansion was therefore like a game; a maze. A maze where there were clues hidden in different locations and you had to find all of them to escape; "escape", in his context, meant not dying.

It meant avoiding a mysterious murder or suicide like the previous owners, for both him and his family. He was convinced that the person who built the house was a mad genius; someone crazy but smart, like P.T. Barnum; and he was going to be the first owner to find the truths hidden within the mansion. He was going to be the first one to conquer the Madhouse, to "win" the game.

BRIDGES

"Hi Giselle, I'm Ken Bridges." The distinguished looking lawyer wearing a bowtie stood up from behind the ornate wooden desk in his law office. A hanging sign said "Bridges & Sons" outside the arched window that overlook the street below.

"Hello," she shook his hand.

"Please, have a seat," he said, pointing to an upholstered and well-worn brown leather chair.

"Thank you." She sat down in front of his desk.

"My paralegal Shirley told me that you're concerned about your husband. Possibly considering a separation?" he asked.

"Yes, I met George in Chicago. We were students at Northwestern but then we got together again during his divorce. He had a bit of a drinking problem."

"Were you married before too?" he asked, taking out a yellow legal notepad and jotting things down with a black fountain pen.

"No," she said. "George and I had Melissa, that's our nine-year-old daughter, back in Chicago. We just moved to Salem last year."

"Tell me about his previous marriage and divorce," he said.

"They were married about ten years, as well. And to hear him say it, his ex-wife was crazy."

"They always are, right?" he smirked, writing down notes.

"Yes, well, he went through a bruising custody battle in Chicago. For his twin teenage daughters."

"And how did that turn out?" the lawyer asked.

"He got biweekly visitations."

"That's usually because the judge thinks the father is unfit," he said.

"I think his drinking was the problem."

"Ok," he said. "And you moved into the Ropes Mansion here last year, right?"

"Yes, that's right," she said, nodding.

"We didn't handle the real estate closing, did we?"

"No, another firm that the real estate agent suggested did," she said.

"You mentioned George's drinking problem. Does he still drink?"

"No," she said. "I want to be clear about that. As far as I know, George hasn't had a drop of alcohol since before Melissa was born. He swears to me that is true, and I have no reason to doubt him. However, I cannot rule out...drugs."

"Drugs?" He stopped writing and looked up at her over his glasses.

"I have no suspicion of anything specific. I never found a trace of anything, not a joint, hell, not even a cigarette in the trash. But I noticed so many odd things about his behavior and mood."

"Ok," said the lawyer, folding his hands on the desk. "By the way, before we go further, I want to give you a little background of my own, if that's ok?"

"Yes, please, I'm sorry, I just started prattling on."

"No, it's ok, really. I've been a lawyer here in Salem for nearly forty years. This law firm," he said, pointing at the plush room around him," has been in my family for six generations. This building, in fact, was built by my grandfather's grandfather. My father retired, and I have been slogging along ever since."

"It's very nice," she said demurely.

"I practice in all different areas, but mostly I focus on family law. I find it to be the most challenging, but also the most rewarding. Helping people has been my family's creed since forever. After my wife passed away from breast cancer ten years ago, I put all my energy into that now. I plan on retiring soon to Florida."

"Thank you," she said. "I really do appreciate you meeting with me, and I'm sorry for your loss."

"Mrs. Lawson, anything you tell me during this meeting is highly confidential and privileged. Sacred, in fact. Under the law of the Commonwealth, whatever you divulge to me in here is the same as being in confession with a priest. I cannot be forced to tell the police, not George, not the judge or jury—no one—what you tell me. And by the way, I'm *your* lawyer. Not George's, not even Melissa's lawyer. So, if you need something, anything, you tell me, and I'm duty-bound to help you and you alone, ok?"

"Yes, I understand," she sighed in relief.

"So, back to your husband," he said.

"I think George is losing his mind," she said. "As I said before, I've never seen a hint of drugs or alcohol. George is healthy and active. He jogs ten miles a week, works out, he is in great shape. But it's his mental state that worries me."

"Has he ever hit you?" the lawyer asked gingerly.

"Never!" said Giselle. "He never even spanked Melissa as a baby."

"Ok, so no drinking, no violence and no specific evidence of drug usage. Tell me about the mental issues."

"So, it all started when he visited Salem last summer without me. He had a business trip here, and he just comes home in Chicago and announces that he bought a house. I never even saw it before we moved in."

"Quite a purchase to make without telling your wife of ten years," he said.

"Yes, and he told me recently that he paid for it entirely with our retirement savings."

"Tell me more about that," he said gravely and writing emphatically.

"Well, he apparently overbid on the place, and then withdrew our entire 401(k) and IRA to pay for it. He didn't wait until we sold our house in Chicago."

"Did he pay it back? Was it a loan against the retirement accounts?"

"He said he put it all back, but I don't think he can. We are getting hit with a huge tax penalty now, and I had no say in any of it."

He scribbled more on his pad. "Ok, go on."

"After we moved in, I discovered that he put ownership of the house in his own name. That's how I was able to avoid coming to the real estate closing. He now owns the mansion, with all of my retirement savings."

The lawyer looked serious. "That is a serious breach of trust. Illegal, too."

"After we moved in, he started acting stranger. He obsessively did a bunch of research, drove to Cambridge and talked to some professor. He started becoming crazy about the history of the house."

"It has quite a long history, nothing unusual in studying up on it, no?"

"He believes it was cursed by Tituba."

"I'm sorry, come again?" he asked.

She repeated herself. "He believes it was cursed by Tituba. The slave, from the witch trials?"

"What makes him think that?" he asked.

"They found her body in the cellar."

"I thought that was you! When I saw your name on my calendar and your address, I knew that something like that had happened from the news and I meant to ask you about it."

"The whole thing was a nightmare, to be honest. George set up an alarm system after the house was vandalized. The first night, the smoke alarm went off. The firemen found a fire behind the wall in the basement and discovered her bones."

"Are they sure it was her? I only read about it in the newspapers, and they never said anything about her."

"No, they aren't really sure. They know the bones are old, but the museum and scientists can't really confirm who they belong to. But then George found voodoo stuff in the garden that he is convinced came from her."

"Wow," he said. "I'm sorry, I don't want to sound unprofessional, but I must say, Mrs. Lawson, that is quite a story. Anyone who lives in *that* house, under those circumstances, might be under quite some stress. Are you sure that he might not just be exhausted, maybe? Overwhelmed?"

"There's more," she said. "He claims he has seen and heard things.

In the house. Ghosts. Voices. Doors opening and closing, that kind of thing. But I have never seen a single thing."

"I have always been a skeptic," he said. But your house is three hundred years old. Can we really say with certainty that he didn't see or hear things that go bump in the night? I mean, we *are* in Salem," he emphasized, pointing up at the grim portraits of his ancestors on the walls.

"Maybe you're right," she said, deflated. "I'm not saying I don't love him or trust him. Of course, I do. But after he drove his car into the ocean—"

"He what?" the lawyer looked up again from his legal pad.

"He says he lost control of our car and it slid down the pier by our house, into the water. The car sunk and was wrecked. He was ok, but I really think he may have hallucinated or something."

"Was he taken to the hospital?"

"Yes," she said. "They found nothing wrong with him."

"Did they happen to do a urinalysis, breathalyzer or blood test? To look for drugs or alcohol."

"Yes, he was totally clean. They even did an MRI. Normal. I talked to the doctor myself."

"Ok, so let's recap," he said, flipping back to the first page of his notepad.

"George is what, 50?"

"Yes, he just turned 50."

"Ok, so we have a 50-year-old white male who is a recovering alcoholic on his second family. Mid-life crisis. Decides on a whim to cash in the retirement accounts and buy a mansion without telling his second wife. Some of us buy expensive boats," he pointed to a framed photograph of a yacht on his desk, "and others buy ridiculous old houses. He drags you across the country to a new town, where you know absolutely no one, is that right?"

"Yes, that's right," she said.

"No friends, no family support structure, in the middle of the witch capital of the world. He suddenly becomes obsessed with ghosts, witches, and goblins. Lo and behold, you find a historically significant skeleton walled up in your basement. Without any evidence of drugs, alcohol, violence, mental or neurological illness, Mrs. Lawson, I'm afraid you have yourself a husband with terrible judgment. He may be acting bizarrely, and I'm not a marriage counselor, but maybe that's what you guys need. A good marriage counselor, that is. I can give you a referral."

"Maybe," Giselle said. "I don't know."

"Ok, the only thing I can add here is that his conduct in withdrawing your retirement savings was illegal. He had no right to access your funds. There will be tax consequences, and those may be significant. But only you can decide if that is enough to justify a divorce or separation. I cannot tell you that."

"I understand," she nodded.

"And it's possible that he has some psychological condition that is not being picked up by tests. Some of us start demonstrating quirks in our older years that can be serious issues masquerading. I have friends in their sixties that are already showing early signs of dementia and Alzheimer's. It runs in families. I don't mean to alarm you or suggest anything like that. Plus, you said the MRI was normal. I'm not a doctor, obviously. But I'm just not sure what legal advice I can give you. Maybe George needs a psychiatrist, I don't know."

"Ok," she said, clutching her purse.

"There's no charge for our consultation today. But here is what I advise, as a lawyer. Start taking detailed notes. Write down all the specific things that George says or does, time of day, details."

"What will that accomplish?" she asked.

"Three things," he said, counting on his fingers.

"First, you might be able to figure out if his actions are predictable or not. Do they happen mostly on weekends? Late nights? That might suggest a pattern to drug use that wasn't picked up by the hospital tests. Look in the trash cans, bottom of the garbage. Sometimes people will stash the incriminating stuff all the way at the bottom. If you find any strange pills or other evidence of drugs, have it tested."

"Ok," she said.

"Second, having detailed notes might give you some insight into something else, like maybe he is eating something that's causing a weird reaction. Maybe taking some vitamin supplement? You said he is into fitness. Maybe he started taking some crazy protein powder. Who knows?"

And third, it will give you ammunition if things get worse, and you need to come back to talk to me again."

"Ammunition, for what?" she asked.

"For another bruising custody battle for George, I'm afraid."

CONFESSION

"I'm...having some big problems at work. With Mark and the rest of the team," said George as he stood at the kitchen island, sipping seltzer.

"Oh God, what next?" asked his exasperated wife. "What happened now?"

"Nothing, that's exactly the problem. Nothing happened. I'm so used to work getting done, you know. Back in Chicago, I had three, four, even five projects a year get completed. Here, I spend my entire life on one crappy project, and if the City Planner doesn't like me, that's it. You're finished."

"I don't understand what you're talking about," she said. "Honestly, I have no clue."

"What am I saying, Giselle, is that this is a different culture here."

"No shit, Sherlock," she said, laughing derisively. "The head of the PTA here is a witch. I mean, a real witch, like she wears the pointy hat and Glenda shoes."

"Well, yeah, but I don't even mean the nuts in Salem. I mean Boston. It's an old boys club. If you didn't go to Harvahd," he said mocking the accent, "you're screwed. Northwestern might as well be community college to these blue bloods."

"You moved us here, George. I told you, I had never even been to Massachusetts. And from what I can tell, you have a point about the old boy network. Families have been here for five, six, seven generations. It's not like Chicago, where everyone's an immigrant. This place has rules, and we are new to the game. But honestly, what did you expect? Boston is like, what, four hundred years old?"

"Yeah, I know," he said, defeated. "I guess I thought that the history was intriguing and novel. I never realized that the history itself can be so oppressive."

"Maybe we just need time, George. Give it some more time, isn't that what you've been telling me all year?"

"Yeah, plus it's this house. It's just like, my mind always drifts back to it. I'm convinced there's something here that I need to figure out. Some puzzle, I can't explain it."

"Can I ask you something? Seriously?" she asked.

"What?"

"Are you taking drugs?" she asked him apprehensively.

"Drugs? What are you talking about?"

"You've done some strange things, you have to admit. I mean, you bought this house and depleted our retirement accounts, dug up the yard, drove off a pier, found a dead body, now work problems, what am I supposed to think?" she asked, starting to cry.

"Oh honey, no, I would never do anything like that, don't you know me? I'm Mr. Health nut, I only drink water and eat granola, for God's sake."

"I know! That's why I'm so confused."

"No, never. I told you that, and I meant every word. Whatever we are going through is completely natural. Just growing pains, I guess." He gave her a hug and a kiss. "I admit it was impetuous for us to move here, but my intentions were good," he said.

"I can't support us living here on my lousy salary alone. Property taxes alone here are brutal, you know that. And even a full-time job at the gym doesn't offer affordable health benefits. You need to support us, George."

"Yes, I know," he said quietly.

"So what are you going to do about work?" she asked, sniffling.

"I guess I'll talk to Mark tomorrow. The problem is that this is the best firm in the city. If I quit or God forbid, get fired, I don't know what other firms would consider hiring me. I'll be a pariah if they think Mark and I had a falling out, you know?"

"How about taking a break? From work, I mean."

"No way, I haven't been there long enough. I think I need to just get this project done, and then go from there."

Giselle nodded. "Oh, one more thing," she said. "I totally forgot. The other day, Detective Tony left us a weird message on the voicemail. He said that they tested the bones you found in the yard, and they weren't animal bones. They were actually that woman's finger bones."

"What the hell?" he said. "How is that possible?"

"I have no clue, and frankly, it's the least of my concerns. Feel free to call him back if you want."

"I will, thanks," he said.

The next day, George arrived at work early but unsure if his office was still going to be there. He put his bag down and saw Mark walking down the hall.

"Hey, come in here and close the door," Mark said to him. George walked in and stood there, not sure what to expect.

"What happened, man? You and Giselle fighting or something?"

"What do you mean," George asked.

"You showed up at work yesterday morning looking like the cat dragged you in. Your eyes were all bloodshot and had dark bags under them. And you smelled weird, like you were out smoking or drinking all night. Then you go off on the city guy which totally screwed us over with him."

"Mark, I'm really sorry," George said. "You have to understand. When I was in Chicago, I worked fifteen-hour days. I drew up plans for four or five projects simultaneously. Here, you guys take your sweet time, and it's a totally different culture."

"No kidding, that's why I hired you. When I called your references, they said that they would need to hire three to four engineers to re-place you. They weren't kidding, you're a rock star. I'm just sorry you feel bored here. Maybe we need to give you more work, more projects. Would that help?"

"I think so. I just want to get motivated, to feel good about my work," George said.

"No problem, if you want more, I can find you more. I have to be honest, man, I have never once had an employee complain that they wanted more crap to do." They laughed out loud.

"Yeah, well, I'm glad we talked. So, what about Friedman?" asked George.

"I already talked him off the ledge. Convinced him that Boston was screwing him over again, which isn't entirely untrue, you know. What you said about patronage and diversity was right. These city guys pull it all the time. They claim they want to give the jobs to diverse firms, but they never do. It's just a way for them to get vendors to kill and underbid each other. The diverse firms never get the work anyway. It's all an evil ruse."

"Hey, I have an idea," said George. "Why don't we hire more diverse engineers? Won't that help make it harder for them to screw our clients over if we have a really good, diverse team?"

"Now you're talking, my man. I will put you in touch with our Diversity Coordinator. See, that's what I like about you. You're a go-get-ter. When you insulted the City, everyone in that room agreed with you. But we don't have the guts to say it or do anything about it except com-plain. You can turn this lemon into lemonade. Let me set up a meeting with Friedman, tell him your idea. Let's take the bull by the horns, ok?"

"Sounds great, man. And by the way, thank you. I really appreciate it."

"No problem," said Mark. "Let's get lunch later."

Mark felt good after their conversation. He was going to get more work to do, which was both exciting and daunting. But when he got back to his office, he started searching the Internet for websites discussing necromancy and what went wrong with the ritual.

SEARCH

"Detective? This is George Lawson, from the Ropes."

"I expected you to call sooner. I called you two days ago and left a message for you to call me back."

"Yeah, sorry. I've been distracted at work. I did get your message, what's up?"

"You tell me," said the detective.

"I'm sorry?"

"We tested the two bones that you say you found buried in your garden under two feet of soil, in a sealed box. Now, I'm told by my lab that they came from the dead slave walled up in the basement."

"I have no idea how that's possible," said George. "Are you sure?"

"Yes, positive match on the DNA. I've got a theory; you want to hear it?" asked the detective coyly.

"Sure," George said. "I'd love to."

"I'll need you to come down to the precinct for me to explain it."

"What?" George laughed. "On television, whenever a cop says that, it means you're going to be arrested or something like that. Am I under arrest?"

"I prefer to talk in person and since you live down the street, and I assume you don't want me coming by your place unannounced."

"I'll be there in 10 minutes," replied George.

He threw on a sweater and walked down to the police station without telling his wife where was headed. Tony was waiting for him in the same conference room he and Giselle had met with him in earlier. This time, he had two other detectives with him that George didn't recognize.

"Come in, George, have a seat again," Tony said.

"Thanks. So, what's this theory?" asked George, sitting down.

"First, I want to know why you lied to me," he asked pointedly.

"What? What are you talking about?" asked George, confused.

"I think you found that dead body and walled it up. I think you were screwing around down there in your basement and set off a smoke detector by mistake and the firemen discovered the little ritual chamber you built."

"What are you talking about?" asked George. "I really am totally confused."

Tony walked over to the window holding a coffee cup and looked out. "I've been going over it again and again in my head since that night. There's just no way that the skeleton's finger bones ended up in your garden. It's physically impossible unless she was murdered back in 1700, chopped up, her little fingers buried in one place, and her body and skull put in another. And you said yourself the wall was newer. Much newer, like hundreds of years more modern. I think you put in that wall yourself and tried to make it look original, and you accidentally set off the smoke alarm doing some ritual behind it. You're an engineer, you can do stuff like that. In fact, I think you bought that house for some weird reason."

"Tony, I'm frankly stunned. Not only at your crazy theory, but let me ask you a question, and I'm no lawyer, but, even if I did what you claim, would that even be a crime?"

"So you admit it?" Tony looked at one of the other detectives who jotted something down on a notepad.

"Absolutely not, I'm just asking what my rights are," said George.

"I think you need a lawyer to answer that question. But let me say this. The Commonwealth has specific laws about how to handle unidentified human remains. If you were playing around with those old bones, it might be a crime. And it certainly was a crime if you lied to me during an investigation about it."

George couldn't believe it. "I really have no idea what you're talking about. But I assure you, that I wouldn't have brought you those things to test that you're say are her finger bones, if I was hiding something like that."

"A fair point, so let me ask you this," said the detective. "Can we look around your basement again? Just to satisfy our curiosity and dispel my crazy theory?"

"No," said George emphatically. "You can't."

"Why not?" asked the detective who was growing even more suspicious now.

"Because you're calling me a liar and accusing me of things I didn't do, things I didn't even remotely think of doing. And I just don't trust you anymore. I have no idea if I let you in my house, if you'll plant evidence or something."

"Well, that's interesting," said the detective. "When you didn't return my call, I was even more convinced my theory was right. So, I happen to already have a search warrant for your basement, since we have probable cause that you committed obstruction of justice."

"What? This is nuts," declared George. "Don't you guys have anything better to do with your time? Like dealing with serious crimes?"

"As we speak, uniformed officers are already executing it at your house," said another detective.

"This is a total abuse of process. Am I free to leave now?" asked George, defiantly. "I'm consulting a lawyer and suing the hell out of all of you."

"You aren't under arrest...yet," said Tony. "So, you can leave. But if you further interfere with the execution of the search warrant or the ongoing investigation, I will remind you that is a misdemeanor and could even be a felony."

"I'm going home," announced George.

George opened the door and walked as quickly as possible out of the front of the police station and home. When he arrived, there were three police cars double parked outside and uniformed officers carrying things out to the car in clear plastic bags.

Giselle was standing outside the front door with her hand over her mouth. "Jesus, George, I want to know right now what is going on," she demanded.

"I wish I knew," he said, running up to her. "Just stay out of it. I went down and talked to Tony. There's some crazy misunderstanding. You know the bones you thought were a parakeet's? The ones I found in the box in the garden?"

"Yeah," she said.

"They were Tituba's. The slave's. In the basement. They belonged to her."

"I don't get it," said Giselle.

"Me neither," said George.

"But why are the police back? They knocked and said they have a warrant to search the basement again. They just came in and started snapping pictures and taking things out of there."

George walked into the house to see what was going on. Two uniformed officers were standing at the entrance to the basement. "Sorry, we can't let you interfere with the search," said one of them apologetically. "Do you need something?"

"I'm not interfering," said George, holding his hands up. "I just want to see what they are taking out of my basement."

"You'll get an inventory list when they are through," said the other officer.

"Yeah, but I just want to see what's happening," George said, ignoring them and walking down the stairs. The cops looked at each other but didn't stop him.

When he went downstairs, he discovered a plainclothes officer was taking photographs of the back room where he had conducted the ritual. He was particularly focused on the bench, the occult books, and the fresh chalk markings on the dirt floor. It appeared that the police had breached the door by clipping the padlock.

George now realized the gravity of the situation. Tony's theory would now seem a lot more plausible. George had re-drawn the circle on the floor and was clearly conducting occult rituals in the same exact location where the ashes and bones had been found. But now it looked like he had planted the skeleton and the bones in the garden first. As bizarre at the situation was, he needed a lawyer to straighten it all out.

CONFLICT

After walking upstairs to the kitchen, George snatched his iPhone. He didn't want Giselle to hear his conversation. He clicked on the Safari application and searched for Salem Massachusetts defense lawyers in Google. He was brought to the first listing which was the Bridges & Sons law firm.

He clicked on the hyperlink, and it autodialed the firm. A receptionist answered.

"Law Office, may I help you?"

"Yeah, my name is George Lawson," he whispered. "I would like to speak to an attorney about a possible criminal case against me."

"Ok, let me see if Mr. Bridges is available."

"Thank you," he said. When he peeked into the foyer, three officers were apparently wrapping up their search and carrying several boxes and bags of evidence out of the house's front door.

"Yes, may I help you?" asked the voice of an elderly man on the phone.

"Yes, hi, my name is George Lawson. My home was just the subject of a search warrant by the Salem police department. I'd like to speak to an attorney about my rights."

"Are you related to a Giselle Lawson?"

"Yes, that's my wife. Why? How do you know her?"

"I'm not at liberty to say. But unfortunately, I'm not permitted to continue this conversation. My receptionist can offer you referrals, or you can call the Massachusetts Bar Association. Good day." He abruptly hung up.

George felt like he was in a surreal dream. Nothing was making sense. He walked into the foyer and saw Giselle standing outside the front door looking horrified. She was watching the police carry out all kinds of evidence that she didn't recognize.

"George, what is all that stuff? I saw a book called 'Mastering Witchcraft' and some gold things that looked like they were from church. Was that yours? Why was that stuff in the basement?"

"Uh, I found some of them, and I bought that book. Up the street. Is that a crime?"

"I have no idea what is going on, George. I'm totally lost."

"Is that why you called a lawyer?" he asked.

"What?" she asked.

"Are you working for Tony? Are you testifying against me for the police or something?"

"George, what the hell are you talking about?"

"Let's see, Giselle. First, you told Dr. Teefey that I was hallucinating. Then you accused me of doing drugs. Then I get called up by Tony, who accused me of God knows what. Finally, I call a defense lawyer, and he says he met with you and that he isn't allowed to talk to me."

"What?" asked Giselle uncomfortably.

"Bridges. I just called their law firm up to ask about the search warrant. The lawyer told me he knew you and couldn't talk to me. Conflict of interest."

She broke down. "I was just worried about Melissa, George. I talked to him so I could figure out how to protect her in case something went wrong. Something like this!" she said, pointing at the police cruisers outside their house and the policemen walking up to them to load them up with George's possessions.

One of the uniformed officers walked up to them and said, "Mr. and Mrs. Lawson, here is a detailed inventory of what we have taken and labeled. It looks like about 33 items. Can you please initial here?"

"Uh, fine, whatever." George scrawled his signature on the form.

"Here's your copy," said the officer, tearing a yellow copy off and handing it to him. George grabbed it. "Bring it to Court with you. Have a good day," the officer said, walking back down the path to his patrol car.

"I don't even know what I'm accused of!" George yelled at the cop. "I haven't done a God damn thing! I haven't touched a drop of booze. I haven't done any drugs. I haven't stolen anything, I haven't lied, nothing!"

"Listen George. I'm so worried about you," said Giselle. "Maybe you should see a psychiatrist and a lawyer."

"A shrink? What the...Giselle, did you hear what I just said. I haven't done anything wrong. Nothing at all."

"So, explain the slave's body in the basement, and her finger bones in the garden," she said, crossing her arms. "You didn't put them there?"

"No! Why and how would I have done that? Didn't you see me cracking open the wax seal? It was under the earth for a century or more. How could I have faked that? *Why* would I have faked that?"

"I don't know. But how did you smell smoke that night?"

"I don't know, I just did. So what?"

"And what were you doing down there? I mean, what is all that stuff in your weird little workshop?"

"Can I be honest?" he asked.

"Oh my God, please. Please," She begged.

"I was trying to contact Tituba."

"What?" she laughed nervously.

"I was trying to speak to her spirit. I spoke to some crazy person with pink hair at a bookshop down the street. They said if I said some weird words and lit some candles, maybe I could figure out how to fix this Godforsaken house," he said, pointing up at the ceiling. "I just wanted to protect you guys. To protect you from whatever bad stuff might happen to us if we stayed here. That's all I ever wanted. I never wanted to hurt anyone."

"So, this is how you do that?" she asked angrily. "You ticked off the police, you hide all kinds of things from me? What will Melissa think when she hears house got searched? Do you think this will help her make more friends at school?"

"I don't know. I feel like my life is coming apart, and I can't even figure out why," he said. "Am I dreaming?"

"No, this isn't a dream, George. It's a nightmare. I really think you need some serious help."

"Ok, ok." he said dejectedly. "I will speak to a shrink, if you think I need to."

Giselle was relieved. "So, what do we do about this?" she said, as the police cruisers pulled away.

"I need a lawyer. I have no idea what any of this means," he said, holding up the yellow police form. "I honestly have no idea what crime they can say I ever committed."

"I don't know, George. But I'm trying to be on your side here. We are a team," she said, putting her arms around him. "I know you mean well, but things have gotten completely out of control in our lives. We can't live like this any longer."

"I agree with you," he said.

The next night, he screamed out loud suddenly and woke up Giselle up. She woke out to find him in bed sitting up, holding the iPad screen in awe, and she asked him what happened. He claimed he had heard a voice and seen a face in the plaster molding moving on the stairs.

She saw nothing.

"You don't see it? Look!" He played the video back again. "It's right there!"

"George, I don't see anything. "Let's go back to sleep, please, don't wake Mel up."

"Let me rewind it again…" he said, tapping the iPad furiously. "I don't see it now. I'm telling you; something weird is going on here. I'm going to get to the bottom of it."

He took a sip of water and laid back in bed. He fully intended to get to the bottom of it.

CONSULTATION

"Hello, George, how are you today?" Dr. Mannu, a gray-haired bearded psychiatrist, stood up in his office and shook George's hand.

"Fine, thank you," said George. "Do I lay down on a couch or something? Stare at the ceiling and talk about my mother?" The doctor laughed.

"I can't tell you how many times new patients ask me that. I don't even have a couch," he said. "Just this old comfy chair. Have a seat," he said, pointing a well-worn brown leather chair.

"Thanks," George sat down and sunk into the chair. "Thank you for seeing me on such short notice."

"No problem. Doctor Teefey and I have been friends since med school. He sent over his file on you, and I got the other faxes from your wife. Have you ever seen a psychiatrist before?" the doctor asked him.

"Nope," George said, looking around. The office was non-descript with some generic modern art prints hanging on the walls.

"This is a pretty straightforward process, nothing like in the movies," the doctor said. "I'm a medical doctor. Given my rates, the insurance companies won't authorize me to conduct any psychotherapy, so I won't be playing Sigmund Freud here. If we decide you need some therapy, I can give you a referral. But I'm here to diagnose if you have any medical conditions."

"So, you get to decide if I'm certifiably nuts," George said.

"Nuts isn't a clinical term," the doctor joked. "Insurance companies won't pay me for treating a garden variety nut. No, they need to know if there's a diagnosable condition that we need to treat with medication. Most of my patients have clinical depression or anxiety or both. A few have more exotic illnesses. But look, I'm here for you. Let's not get too bogged down with terminology. Also, I should remind you that anything we discuss here is strictly confidential. Just between us."

"My wife thinks I'm losing my mind, Doctor," George exhaled.

"And what do you think?"

"I don't know," confessed George. "I really don't know what is happening to me anymore."

"Tell me why your wife thinks you're not doing well," he took out a notebook and scribbled some notes down. "Or at least what she told you."

"I guess it started back in Chicago. I was bored after I turned 50. I was here on a business trip, and I saw the Ropes Mansion and I just bought it. Like that. Sold all our stocks in the 401(k) and bought it without telling my wife."

"Why do you think you did that?" he asked.

"I guess I felt trapped."

"Any other big decisions like that? Buy any expensive pets? Cheat on your wife? Quit your job?"

"No, not really. But after we moved, I guess I started getting interested in our house's history. It has seen more than its fair share of tragedy over the centuries."

"We'll get back to that. Do you ever use any drugs or alcohol?"

"Nothing. Not a drop or pinch. Trust me, I have had my share of booze."

"Recovering addict?"

"10 years now."

"Congratulations," the doctor said. "That's a serious achievement."

"Thank you. I don't think Giselle, that's my wife, I don't think she recognizes how hard it is for me."

"Feel tempted a lot?"

"Every day," George said. "Every single day. But I always resist."

"Ok, so no drugs or drinking, good." He wrote something down. "Are you currently in any twelve step programs?"

"No. Not anymore. After the move, I guess I started losing my focus at work. Then, they found a skeleton in our basement. That threw me for a loop."

"Yeah, I know all about that. I read the police reports you sent over, as well as the news stories. How has that affected you?"

"I'm afraid for my kid. My wife. Even myself. So many people have died in that house. I believe it is cursed."

"Do you believe you're cursed?" asked the doctor.

"No, well not yet. I believe the house was damned and the curse eventually falls upon the residents. I just wanted peace. So, I started dabbling in the occult to speak to the soul of the woman who died there. I thought maybe I could release her. Somehow, things got totally out of control after that. The police think I lied about her body."

"Did you?"

"Absolutely not. I never said a word that was a lie. I didn't volunteer what I was doing with Giselle, I didn't tell her about the rituals, but I didn't commit any crimes or ever lie," George adamantly insisted.

"I reviewed Dr. Teefey's report that you sent over," the doctor said, flipping through his files. "The word that gave me pause was 'hallucination.' Did you see or hear anything that you now suspect wasn't real?"

"The things I've seen were definitely real. There are some strange things in that house, Doctor. But I'm convinced they are all real."

"Did anyone else see them?"

"I think my dog did," said George.

"Ok, other than the dog. Anyone who can talk?"

"No, I don't think so. But I'm telling you, Doctor, I have seen ghosts. Even at the park."

"You have seen things outside the house?" the doctor asked.

"Yes, at the pier and the park. And I had a car accident."

"I read that in your file too. You said you lost control of your car? Drove it off the pier?"

"It was an electrical malfunction," George said defensively. "I don't think it was my fault."

"Any missing time?"

"What do you mean?" asked George.

"Have you ever found yourself somewhere, and you just couldn't remember how you got there? You know, like a blackout."

"Well, awhile back, I was removing some wallpaper and I think I fainted."

"What happened, exactly? Do you remember anything?"

"I think I just inhaled too much paint thinner because I didn't open the windows. I passed out and woke up many hours later."

"Ok," the doctor said, writing something down. Here's my view. I think you put yourself under tremendous stress. Moving at your age, buying an expensive house without telling the wife. New job, recovering alcoholic without a sponsor in a twelve-step program. Are you having any difficulty sleeping?"

"Yeah, most nights, I'm up half the night. Nightmares. Constant nightmares."

"Sleeplessness contributes to it. It's a vicious cycle. The less we sleep, the more agitated we become. It feeds on itself, until we crash and burn. We see and do some strange things when we are in that mode."

"Right," said George.

"Tell me about the nightmares," asked the doctor.

"They aren't anything too specific that I can recall," George said. "They're not the same recurring theme, but when I wake up, I feel paralyzed. I'm in a cold sweat. I can't get back to sleep, so I toss and turn all night. When my alarm goes off, I'm in hell and drag myself to work."

"Ok," said the doctor. "So, my medical diagnosis, at least preliminarily, is that this is environmental. At 50, most people don't suddenly develop symptoms of paranoid schizophrenia or organic diseases that cause profound hallucinations. Your MRI was perfect, so I don't suspect early Alzheimer's or dementia. Ruling out drugs and alcohol, that leaves us with only environmental causes like stress and anxiety. And you fit those criteria, given your decisions."

"So, I'm not nuts?" George joked.

"I honestly don't think so. At least I don't see evidence of anything that would neatly fit DSM-IV criteria for anything serious."

"I guess that's a relief. Sorta, anyway," said George.

"Yeah, it doesn't give much comfort because you still have to deal with all this...stuff," the doctor said, flipping through the thick file. "You still have the criminal charges pending, right?"

"Yeah," George said. "What a pain in the ass."

"I don't doubt it. But let a good lawyer deal with that. So tell me more about work."

"I work in the city. At a top engineering firm. It's been stressful. The culture is so different from Chicago. But I'm keeping it together, for now, but I'm not sure for how much longer. My boss and I had some words, but he has been understanding. I just don't know. If I keep screwing up, I will probably get axed eventually."

"Ok, here's what I propose," said the doctor, taking out his prescription pad. "I can write you some scripts to get you back on your feet. I don't have a hard diagnosis to give you, but I can probably call it something like mood disorder not otherwise specified or generalized anxiety disorder. Even though we know it's situational, I can treat it until you feel better, ok?"

"Ok, great," George said. "So, what does that mean exactly? Treat it?"

"I will give you some anti-anxiety medication. They're to be taken 'as needed,' ok?"

"What's that mean?" George asked.

"I wouldn't take them every single day. I don't think the situation warrants that, yet. You should just take one when you're feeling particularly stressed out. I will also give you something to help you get a good night's sleep. Once you get through a couple of stable weeks, I predict you'll feel good as new."

"Thank you so much, Doctor."

"Of course, you're already not drinking, but definitely stay off alcohol or other drugs while taking these things. Otherwise, your head might explode."

"Not a concern, Doc. It was nice talking to you. Really, I mean it. I feel like I'm on the right track now."

"Glad I could help. One more thing. After the dust settles, and I'm not saying you need it, I can give you the names of some local therapists. They can work wonders in treating middle-aged anxiety, which we all suffer from now and then." The doctor smiled. "I also think you might went to get back into the habit of AA meetings."

"Thanks, I may do that," George said.

"Ok, let's see each other in a month, just to check in, ok?"

"Perfect, thank you."

PILLS

After seeing the psychiatrist, George stood at the pharmacy, waiting for his prescriptions to be filled. The girl working behind the counter handed him a white paper bag and asked him if he had any questions about taking the medications. "No, not really, I guess," he said, taking the bag. But he had many questions.

He had never taken prescription psychiatric medication before and wasn't sure what to expect. Dr. Mannu had been nonchalant about the drugs, but George just wasn't sure what state of mind would legitimately constitute an "as needed" scenario. He just hoped that he'd have the presence of mind to figure that out as he went. He also wasn't sure how to adequately assure Giselle that he was going to be ok.

When he got home, Giselle was waiting for him. Melissa was at a friend's house.

"So, what did the doctor say?" she asked nervously.

"He said I'm basically under tremendous stress and anxiety of my own creation. And my trouble sleeping is taking a toll on my mental health. He gave me sleeping pills and anti-anxiety medication that I can take 'as needed,' whatever that means."

"Well, that's great," she said, sounding relieved. "Did he say anything else?"

"No, not really, he just told me I should be fine in a couple of weeks, once I relax and get some sleep."

"And the hallucinations? Blackouts? Did he have any explanation for those?"

"Not really, he said that it's not drugs, alcohol or schizophrenia. He said it was environmental. That a lot of guys my age can go through stuff like this. Something like that. But he wasn't concerned. He wants to see me in a month to check in. He also thinks I might benefit from therapy and AA meetings again."

"That's great," said Giselle. "I think that's good advice. Maybe then we can get back to some level of normalcy in this family now."

"That's all I want too, honey." He kissed her and wanted to feel positive about their new direction.

That night, right before he went to sleep, he took a sleeping pill with some seltzer. He was out cold within twenty minutes. He fell into a deep sleep but had even more terrifying nightmares. In one, he was drifting out at sea at night in a sailboat by himself. He had no idea how to manage it, and it was rocking and being tossed back and forth by violent waves.

He was isolated, with no one in sight to help. A strong wave struck the hull and knocked him on his back. As he looked up from the deck, he saw the mast snap off and nearly strike him as it fell. He had a feeling of fear and helplessness that was torturing him. He tried to wake up from the dream and yet he couldn't. He felt like he was being smothered. Paralyzed again.

When he finally woke up, he felt horrible. He was groggy; it was like a hangover after a night of heavy drinking. The memories of the dreams were foggy, but he could remember bits and pieces of the terror that permeated his night.

Rather than feeling rested from the sleeping pill, he felt worse today. But he remembered Doctor Mannu's words, that within a couple of weeks, he should start feeling better, and things would start looking up.

"How did you sleep?" asked Giselle in a chipper way when he came down to the kitchen before work.

"Great," he lied.

"Did the sleeping pill help?"

"Yep, I feel great. Thanks for asking."

His eyes were burning, and he had a gnawing ache at the base of his skull. He took a few Advil and looked at the bottle of medication for anxiety that Dr. Mannu had prescribed. He figured he would wait and see if he needed it, so he took it to work with him in his bag.

When he got to his office, his headache was gone. He was numb from the analgesics, but he still felt terrible. He tried to sip some coffee, but it tasted bitter no matter how much milk and cream he added. The only thing he could get down was his seltzer.

Mike walked into his office. "Hey man! How's the new Garibaldi hotel project going?"

"What?" George asked, rubbing his bloodshot eyes.

"Uh, the hotel. We discussed it last week. Remember?" Mike pointed at the thick unopened file on George's desk.

"Oh right, right. I haven't dug into it yet."

"Jesus, are you kidding? We have a meeting with the client at 3, he is expecting a total workup of the schematics. Please don't tell me you don't have them…"

"I will, I will. I just need to crank. Give me a couple of hours."

Mike nervously walked out of George's office and closed the door behind him.

George tried to work on the designs using his desktop computer, but the screen looked blurry. He tried re-booting it several times, but nothing seemed to help.

"Damn it," he said under his breath. "Now's not the time," he said, smacking the monitor.

He took his laptop out of his bag, but it wouldn't boot up until it installed several updates. The screen said it would take over an hour to install. George was starving but didn't have enough time to eat lunch.

He looked up at the clock on his desk and realized that he only had two hours left before the meeting. He looked down into his bag and saw the prescription pill bottle. He figured that maybe he should take two, given how much anxiety he was feeling. He grabbed his water bottle and took large gulps to wash the pills down.

When he walked into the conference room ten minutes late, the client was waiting with Mike and the rest of the team.

"Sorry I'm late. I just wanted to finish this thing up. It was taking me so long, I had to get ahead. You know?"

"Uh, ok George," said Mike nervously. "Shall we jump right in?"

"Sure, sure," said George, fumbling with his power cord clumsily. "It's still updating. Let's leave the door open so I can be comfy." Mike stared at him.

George flopped down in a black leather conference chair, without introducing himself to the client. "Man am I hungry," he said.

"I'm John Garabaldi," said a distinguished looking man in a suit standing up to shake George's hand.

"Oh, hi hi," said George. "Sorry, I should've introduced myself. John, I'm the man who is going to make your dreams come true."

Mike laughed nervously. "Hah, George is from Chicago. He's new to the team, he just joined us late last year. We're all excited to see what he put together for you."

"Ok, here we go," said George, turning on the overhead screen. Everyone turned to look at it.

George's PowerPoint presentation was filled with strange drawings and images from the Salem Witch Trials. Random words of text were in bullet points: "*What do people want? Death. Carnage. Mayhem.*"

"And this is where I live," George said, pointing a photograph of the Ropes Mansion. "Salem. Witch Capital of the World, we call it. That's what it is. Full of witches," he laughed. "There's my house. There's the museum."

The team members each looked at each other, wondering where George was going with this bizarre display.

George continued. "John, you're building a hotel in Boston, right? So, my idea…is forget that. Transport the entire project to Salem. We can build you a hotel that is all about witches. Appeal to the tourists. Imagine the merchandising. Huh? Am I right guys?"

"George," Mike interrupted. "We're waiting for see the specifications for the hotel plans. You were going to work up the way the Boston public utility system and harbor roadway are going to intersect with the new harbor hotel. We aren't interested in Salem or weird marketing ideas."

"Oh, that. Yeah, well, that's not my focus anymore. My focus is in Salem now."

"Mike, what's going on here," asked John Garibaldi. "I don't have time for joking around. I have a hard stop at 4, and a flight to Denver to catch."

"I understand. Let me talk to George for two minutes outside, ok?"

George and Mike walked outside the conference room door. George was glassy eyed.

"Are you drunk? High?" demanded Mike, trying to keep his voice down so the others inside the room couldn't hear him.

"Nope, I'm doing just great," said George, making the OK sign with his fingers. "What, you guys don't like my ideas? A Witchcraft hotel? Brilliant marketing, I think. Salem Chamber of Commerce would eat it up. Hell, I might build it myself."

"What happened to the schematics you were working on this morning?" demanded Mike.

"I guess I got distracted," George said casually.

"George..." Mike stammered.

"Yep?" George said with a smile.

"You're fired. Get your shit and get out. Now."

"Pfft. Whatever." George said, strolling briskly back to his office to grab his bag and his pills.

REDUX

I t was Halloween again. For Giselle, it was a bit weird to think that it had already been a full year since the last one. Salem was still the same; almost exactly the way it was last year. Maybe even more pronounced in its way of life.

When Giselle looked outside the window, it seemed like there were even higher scores of people than those that had shown up for Halloween the year before, and this time in more detailed and exotic costumes. She thought about how she had dressed up last year, too, happily taking part in the revelry. It was a fun thing to do, at the time.

But Giselle wasn't wearing a costume today. She was the one looking outside the window, watching the people, and sighing in exhaustion and sadness, her sorrow drawn from the very memory she had just cherished. All it took for her life to had changed so drastically, was a year.

She walked towards the front door and called for Melissa, telling her to get ready for trick or treating again. Giselle felt that Melissa, at least, deserved some sort of happiness and normalcy after all the weirdness that had been going on in their household over the past year. As she got closer to the front door, she started to hear a hammering sound, and she stepped outside only to find George sweating like a construction worker, banging furiously on stakes to install bizarre Halloween decorations outside. She stepped out the front door and found that he was trying to nail a giant sign just above the front door with the words "MY MADHOUSE" scrawled on it in red paint to look like blood spatter.

She held her face in her palms. She was tired. George had been nothing but a handful for her over the past few months, and she wasn't sure how much more of this she could take. As the weeks progressed since he had his accident at the pier, he had spent so much money and time, and effort, continuing to add to the elaborate, high-tech security system in their home as though they were preparing for the Purge.

The system was becoming bizarrely sophisticated, transforming the entire house in something a bit like a discount bunker. It even had a panic button, that instantly shut all the doors and windows and locked everything once pushed.

George tested it once in the house, much to Giselle and Melissa's surprise. He shut everything in and had trouble getting everything to open properly again, and they were stuck inside on that day for a total of four hours. George spent weeks building and perfecting that system, and she and her daughter were forced to wake up multiple times to the sound of drilling or hammering or alarms.

She had asked him what the added security system was for, and it was a question she already knew the answer to. It obviously had something to do with the Madhouse again, and how their lives were "at stake" and how they could fall under attack at any moment.

She didn't even recognize him anymore. This wasn't the man that she had fallen in love with, and she didn't think even he realized that. She believed that a person could only be saved if they wanted to; that if someone was sinking in quicksand, you could only pull that person out when they stretched out their hand to you. George wasn't going to stretch out his hand. He wanted to sink, and if she wasn't careful, he was going to take both her and Melissa along with him. She wouldn't allow him to do that. This time he was obsessing on decorating and portraying the house as "His Madhouse."

"...Take it down," she demanded.

George stopped his hammering and turned his head slowly to look at her, a blank and unimpressed look on his face.

"Take it down now, George. I told you not to decorate our house with this sick concept. I can't have all these people looking at my family as if we're crazy. Take the sign down."

George climbed down the ladder and folded it up, lifted it with one arm and headed back inside. He stopped at the door to look her directly in the eye.

"It's already up. You should've come out sooner."

Giselle snapped.

"Fuck you, George. Fuck. You. I've had with you and your bullshit. Your obsession with this house, and everything— all the shit you've been doing around lately. Have you even stopped to think about how all of this makes me feel? About how Melissa feels about all of this? What is this? You have to stop. I'm not having any of it, anymore. You go back outside and take that sign down right now or I swear to God—"

George walked inside and placed the ladder against the wall, while Giselle continued ranting. He had now started struggling to put on a fog making machine, one that he found in the house. It was apparently left over by the previous owner. It wasn't working, and it was starting to make George frustrated, because he needed the fog machine at the entrance to give his Madhouse a spooky feel. It was even worse with Giselle shouting and complaining at him, and soon he and Giselle were locked in a hot, loud argument.

Melissa had come out of her room in her costume, an innocent looking version of Harley Quinn from the DC universe. She found her parents arguing, Giselle screaming at the top of her voice holding George by his shirt and George trying to get her hands off him as he struggled with the fog machine.

Melissa wished she could go back to the days when it was just her, her Mom and Dad living a quiet but happy life in the Midwest, before her Dad became obsessed with a lot of "Salem stuff", as she casually called it.

Her father no longer had time to talk to or play with her and her Mom always seemed so stressed dealing with her Dad. Last Halloween, George snuck her some candy away from Mom and her Mom would eventually catch her but let her keep the candy anyway. It was like a little game they played. They didn't play it anymore. She closed her little eyes to fight back tears and ran out of the house into a crowd full of colorful and exotically dressed tourists and locals.

Giselle had gotten tired of screaming. It was like nothing she said to George was getting through. In fact, throughout their whole exchange, the only thing George was interested in was getting her to leave his shirt alone so he could continue struggling with the fog machine. She got frustrated and screamed and left, and George just kept on trying the machine anyway. She sat outside for a while and cried, wondering how her life and marriage had gone so wrong. All she really had left now was Melissa—

Melissa. The thought just came to her mind. She was supposed to go trick or treating with her. She should have been ready a while ago. She dried her eyes quickly and went into Melissa's room to check on her, calling out to her that she was sorry for taking so long as she walked up to the door. She stopped mid-sentence, because she opened the door to Melissa's room, and she wasn't there.

PANIC

She went up and walked around the house, calling Melissa's name. No answer. No Melissa. Melissa was never really the kind of girl to hide from her anyway. She always wanted to stay close to those she cared about. Where was she? did she leave the house? why didn't she tell her? They were supposed to go together. Did she say something wrong? or maybe... did she see her and George arguing?

She ran outside now and called out to her. No answer. Some people simply looked at the woman screaming at the top of her voice for her lost child but looked away and kept on with their revelry anyway. Giselle ran into the crowd frantically, looking around and calling Melissa's name, checking the face of every single young girl she saw that had her back turned to her, much to their parents' disapproval. She didn't care. She needed to find Melissa.

After searching for Melissa around the crowd for a half hour to no avail, Giselle was genuinely gripped with fear. The tears were starting to run down her face, and her voice shook as she screamed Melissa's name, but people simply parted ways for her, feeling sorry for the woman that was crying and calling out the name of her lost child in the middle of Halloween revelry.

She came out of the bulk of the crowd to a parking lot, and two policemen were at the forefront, sharing a corndog. They noticed the wailing woman and ask her what was wrong. She frantically told them that she couldn't find her daughter, and she was worried sick. They told her not to worry and would help her search.

The two police went into two different directions, one of them going with Giselle, while the other went by himself, with Giselle's phone in his hand, and a picture of Melissa on the screen.

They communicated with each other through their radios, sharing information on what streets they had covered. Forty-five minutes had passed since they met Giselle, and there was still no sign of Melissa. It was difficult for the officers to check the face of every little girl they came across, especially because Melissa wasn't the only young girl who decided to wear a Harley Quinn costume this year. The search was tedious and fruitless.

But one officer who went alone made headway. He met a store owner who claimed that he had seen the girl in the picture, she had walked to his store and asked for some cotton candy but was unable to pay. A clown came by and paid for her, asking in return that she play with him. He pointed to an old arcade in the Salem Willows Park that seemed relatively empty for a time when people were gathered in high numbers and claimed that he last saw them going in there.

The uniformed officer ran into the arcade and started calling for Melissa. He had called her name three times when he heard a girl's voice from a corner, and her found her with a clown. They were playing skeeball together.

He picked up his walkie-talkie to tell Giselle and his partner that he found the missing girl, and they were there in a matter of a few seconds. Giselle embraced her daughter with tears in her eyes and thanked the officers. The clown, when questioned, explained that he had asked Melissa what she was doing out there alone and had offered to take her back to her family, but she insisted on not going back home and playing outside instead, because going back home "made her sad."

The game of skeeball was to determine a winner, and if the clown had won then Melissa would have to follow him back to her parents. Giselle apologized to the clown and officers for their time and support, and most especially to her little girl for making her feel unsafe in her own home. They walked back home together, hand in hand, and Giselle thought to share what had just happened with George.

If anything was going to change him at this point, it could only be his daughter, Melissa. He had to change for her. The real victim of everything that had been happening so far, was Melissa. Even George should realize that now. She thought to speak to him when he got back, because she was sure he had also ran out to look for his daughter when he heard her screaming Melissa's name. Giselle came home, however, to meet George still inside, disassembling the fog machine, and muttering to himself.

"... George." she called pensively. He didn't even turn to look at them.

"George, Melissa ran out. She ran away home. She left because of our argument. She was scared of home. I thought you'd be out there looking for her... George? are you listening to me..?"

He waved his hand at her dismissively.

"I said," Giselle growled, her voice and temper rising exponentially, "Melissa was missing, and it was because of us, George! Because of *you*! You need to change for her!"

Unfazed, George looked up from his machine. He stared at them for a while, and then went back to tinkering his fog machine. "If you wanted her to stay inside, then just say so. I can upgrade the security in her room as well."

BREAK

iselle was completely done. That was it. That was as far as it could go. As far as she could go. She felt something snap in her chest as he said that, and it hurt, but it also made her eyes clear. Very clear. She no longer shouted at George. She didn't scream at him. She said nothing. She simply took Melissa by the hand and packed her things. She headed inside the master bedroom and packed some things for herself, and headed out of the house with their bags and her daughter, hopped into the car and drove away. Right there, right then, on Halloween night, Giselle and Melissa left, and George wasn't even aware of their exit until he gave up on the fog machine and stepped outside for some fresh air.

He noticed his car was gone. He didn't hear anything from them inside the house either. He didn't go in to check, but somehow, he knew that they were gone. He could just feel it. The house was huge and empty behind him, and as he stood outside, the cool night breeze brushing against his face, staring up at the starry night sky. He felt, for the first time in a long time, totally empty and purposeless.

Marlena suddenly walked up to say hello to him. Considering the events that just happened in his household, he would have ignored her completely and continued wallowing in his encroaching depression, until he looked down at her and saw what she was wearing.

She was still beautiful, all right, just as beautiful as she was when he first saw her last year, and, this time, she came wrapped in a gift in the form of a costume. It was the same one that Giselle had worn last year; Poison Ivy, the green tights with the bare neck. She was simply oozing with sexiness as she smiled at him and looking at her painfully reminded him of Giselle.

He became overcame with sadness and lust, and lost control of himself, giving into his more primal desires and desperate thinking. He took her by the hand and pulled her inside his house, and tore her clothes right off her body in sexual desperation. He stuffed her breasts in his mouth and filled his hands with her body. Reasoning logically, such an approach was sexual harassment and perhaps even attempted rape, but he didn't care. She didn't stop him, either, or he didn't even notice. Instead, they lay down on the floor right there, behind the front door, and had sex with each other for the first time.

The front door swung open and struck his foot. Giselle had returned home at that very moment, and just happened to have forgotten her purse, one of the few things one should practically never forget whilst leaving your husband and going away to start a new life. Perhaps she had returned to give George one last chance. Perhaps she wanted to see if he had felt their absence; if he finally realized how he had been destroying their family. He didn't know, and would never find out, because Giselle returned to find him on the floor with another woman, wearing the same costume she had worn for Halloween a year before. They looked up at her as she opened the door, and they stared at each other for what seemed like an eternity, even though they said nothing. Giselle broke the stare and walked inside, grabbed her purse and left, but stopped at the door to say to him, "I hope you die in this house."

George was now left sitting on the floor, staring at empty space in the Madhouse, as both his wife and child had left. Marlena had run out of the back door. It was like he was finally thinking straight for the first time in months, but so fast and so suddenly that he couldn't process it all completely. He held his head in his hands and started to scream, his mind spiraling into depression as the events of the past few months start to run through his head, as he slowly realized how he ruined his own life with his own hands. His wallowing and self-hate were interrupted by rattling on the windows by the porch, and he ran to the window to find kids; young revelers from the Halloween events climbing up on his windows again, trying to get inside the famed Madhouse.

He lost his patience and screamed, ran inside his study and pushed the wide red button, the one that acted as a panic button to immediately shut down the whole house. The revelers were caught off guard as the system loudly activated, and those climbing the windows were forced to fall off, sustaining injuries, one of them losing everything after his elbow as one the shields George installed on the windows suddenly ripped through the flesh on his upper arm.

The same policemen who helped find Melissa were quickly alerted by an alarm that George had programmed with an automated message to call the police.

"This is George Lawson. If you are receiving this message, it is because I am going to kill the intruders into my Madhouse. You cannot stop me."

The police received the recurring message over their radios and rushed to the scene where they found a boy bleeding out of his arm screaming in pain, several other kids groaning in pain on the floor, and a crazed man laughing maniacally from a half open window inside the mansion.

They confronted him, asking him to come outside with his hands on his head. George, who was practically insane at this point, and had lost all sense of self, screamed at the policemen approaching him.

He started shouting at them, claiming that he "had evidence", and the police reemphasized for him to quietly surrender himself. George climbed out the half open window and rushed towards one of the policemen, reaching into his back pocket as he lunged.

The officer was startled by his sudden movements and drew his gun and shot George straight through the neck.

Stopped dead in his tracks, George stared at the policeman in shock, before he finally dropped to the floor with his eyes still wide open, releasing the grip on his back pocket to reveal a picture with him, Giselle and Melissa in it.

FINALE

The funeral was short and quiet. It was attended by the locals he had come to know in Salem; Marlena, who worked at the brewery; Tim, the owner of Salem's Ropes Tonic, the old man who worked as a taxi driver around the area, the clown who had helped Melissa, the two policemen who were present at his death, Dr. Mannu and even the boy who had helped George out at the pier when he drove his Tesla straight into the ocean.

Giselle and Melissa were present as well and stood closest to his grave. His first two daughters and ex-wife weren't present, and everyone apart from his immediate wife and child stood farther away. A priest recited a few words and Melissa placed a rose, along with some candy, on her father's coffin. Giselle hugged her as she returned, a somber look on her face. The coffin was lowered.

A month later, Tim stood inside the front lobby of the brewery.

"That was a lively one," he said, using one hand to support himself as he rested on the counter.

"No kidding," replied the cab driver, "I didn't think he'd last that long."

"You know, toward the end," adds Marlena, resting on the counter, "it felt like he started coming back to his senses. Like his feelings for his family overpowered the effects of the Tonic. It's hard to tell, because he died before he could make any certain moves, but it felt like that to me."

"Impossible," said the clown, who walked out from behind the shack, holding a cup of Salem's Ropes Tonic in one hand.

"No one can beat the Tonic. Remember when it was called absinthe? We even upped the dose to make the hallucinations more potent. The Madhouse continues."

"Good thing the thujone in the absinthe doesn't show up on drug tests." Dr. Mannu stepped forward. "He got tested at the hospital after the accident. When I gave him the pills, the interaction made him snap."

"Good work, Doc. But let's not forget how Marlena finished him off fucking him," sneered Tim.

"I do my job well," retorted Marlena, chuckling, "Since fucking him kept him here, that's exactly what I did."

"Speaking of," chipped in the taxi driver, "we didn't get the wife and kid. They never took the Tonic. Doesn't that break a streak?"

"It doesn't matter,", The clown replied, "he's dead. The wife and kid didn't suspect that he was being drugged for a second. They think he lost his mind. The Tonic worked. He got addicted and it messed him up good. Well, add another name added to the Madhouse's list. I bet more get curious and come to investigate the Madhouse now. More business for us."

"Speaking of business," added Tim, pointing at someone approaching the shack, "here comes the new one."

The taxi driver and the clown walked away quickly, while Marlena bobbed up her hair and put on her beautiful smile and fixed her breasts. Tim took out a bottle of his Tonic, and poured it into a plastic cup.

"Hi," greeted the new owner, cheerfully, "I just moved into the house next door. Guess I'm your new neighbor." He chuckled nervously.

"We're happy to have you." answered Marlena, flaunting her killer smile.

"And to commemorate that, here's a drink on me." Tim said, as he stretched a cup of Salem's Ropes Tonic at the new owner.

"I don't know..." The owner replied, rejecting with his hands politely, "I don't really like alcohol and the like."

Marlena took the cup from Tim and took a small sip.

"This isn't alcohol. Just local tonic. That's what we call soda here."

The new owner collected the cup from Marlena and smelled the drink suspiciously. Marlena smiled at him and urged him to try it.

"Go on," she says, with a smile, "just have a taste."

AUTHOR'S STATEMENT

There are several strands in Salem's Ropes (pardon the pun) that are worth mentioning. The first, and most obvious, is that George was unknowingly consuming the active ingredient in absinthe called thujone, by drinking Salem's Ropes Tonic. Thujone is a real substance in wormwood (the common name of some species of artemisia plants) and some other plants, which is purported to have hallucinogenic or psychotropic effects. There are several types of wormwood, and these are used to flavor absinthe, bitters, vermouths, and bitter liqueurs.

Absinthe historically was an alcoholic beverage flavored with grand wormwood (artemisia absinthium), and often anise, fennel, and/or licorice, plus other herbs. It is traditionally high in proof compared with other spirits and is often green (absinthe verte) or clear (absinthe blanche) in color.

In the late 1800s and first years of the 1900s, widespread consumption of absinthe was blamed for many types of societal problems in Europe. A sensational murder blamed on absinthe in Switzerland in 1905, and a campaign by the recovering wine industry after the phylloxera crisis, lead to absinthe bans in Europe and other parts of the world. One author claimed that "[a]bsinthe makes you crazy and criminal, provokes epilepsy and tuberculosis, and has killed thousands of French people. It makes a ferocious beast of man, a martyr of woman, and a

JOSEPH C. GIOCONDA

degenerate of the infant, it disorganizes and ruins the family and menaces the future of the country."[1]

Today, all absinthe and other alcoholic beverages must be "thujone-free" which the United States defines as "[b]ased upon the level of detection of FDA's prescribed method for testing for the presence of thujone, TTB considers a product to be "thujone-free" if it contains less than 10 parts per million of thujone." Other countries have different limits on thujone content.

According to WebMD, "[w]hen taken by mouth, thujone can cause seizures, muscle breakdown (rhabdomyolysis), kidney failure, restlessness, difficulty sleeping, nightmares, vomiting, stomach cramps, dizziness, tremors, changes in heart rate, urine retention, thirst, numbness of arms and legs, paralysis, and death."

Notably, after the accident at the pier, George's blood tests and urinalysis at the Salem Hospital don't reveal the presence of alcohol or drugs, which would include thujone. This is credible because thujone would not show up on a standard drug test. Consequently, if someone like George were to have consumed a large quantity of tonic containing even trace amounts of thujone, he might very well have experienced auditory and visual hallucinations, nightmares and seizures.

Second, George obsessively explores the history of the Salem Witch Trials, including the role of Tituba. Interestingly, even though the 1692 events in Salem are some of the most widely studied events in American history, very little is known about Tituba or her fate by mainstream historians. Arthur Miller has been criticized by some who think his depiction of Tituba was inaccurate, but others believe it is as accurate as we know.

Third, like many residents of Salem, George dabbles in the occult. While thujone consumption would have affected his judgment and perceptions, the rituals that he engages in are real, and contained in modern and medieval texts. I have written extensively about the putative

---

[1] Barnaby, Conrad III. *Absinthe History in a Bottle*. Chronicle Books, 1988.

origins of these occult "grimoires" in my first novel, the Pope's Butcher, which is set in 1486 Europe.

Further, the Ropes Mansion is very real and very beautiful, as are its amazing gardens. Some of the untimely and tragic deaths described in Salem's Ropes occurred in the house. In fact, there are numerous reports that the Ropes Mansion may indeed be haunted. According to many "ghost tours" in Salem, the Ropes Mansion is often called one of the most haunted houses in Salem, which is reputed to have many such houses.

According to legend, the Ropes Mansion is genuinely haunted by the spirit of Abigail who died after her nightgown caught on fire near one of the upstairs fireplaces. Reportedly, Rick and Georgette Stafford, former caretakers of the Mansion, claim to have caught Nathaniel Ropes on film. The image was taken during an insurance appraisal and reveals two hands of a man seated on a couch. Robert Cahill published the photo in Ghostly Haunts, writing that, "Here the judge sits for a spell on the front hall couch. After all, if you were wandering around this mansion for over 200 years, you'd want to sit for a while, wouldn't you?"

The Ropes Mansion is generally open for public tours and is currently maintained by the Peabody Essex Museum. The 1993 film Hocus Pocus was filmed outside its beautiful exterior, so the house has many interested visitors year-round.

Finally, unfortunately, there is no microbrewery near the Ropes Mansion (yet).

BIBLIOGRAPHY

Cawthorne, Nigel. *Witch Hunt: History of a Persecution.* Chartwell Books, 2004.

Miller, Arthur. *The Crucible.* Penguin Books, 1952.

Kunze, Michael. *Highroad to the Stake: A Tale of Witchcraft.* Univ. of Chicago Press, 1987.

Thurston, Robert W. *Witch, Wicce, Mother Goose: The Rise and Fall of the Witch Hunts in Europe and North America.* Pearson, 2001.

CPSIA information can be obtained
at www.ICGtesting.com
Printed in the USA
BVHW041408101021
618593BV00005B/9